THIRST

HELLISH #4

CHARITY PARKERSON

--Warning: This book is intended for readers over the age of 18.

INTRODUCTION

In his twelve hundred years on earth, Baptiste has been called many things. Vampire. Voodoo Priest. Demon mate. They're all true.

Running a small voodoo shop in the heart of the French Quarter has given Baptiste something to do with his free time other than pine for the mate he never sees. While it's true he sells worthless trinkets to tourists, he's also been known to sell a real spell or two. As the child of a powerful Druid, Baptiste already knew all there was to know about the supernatural world before he willingly turned Vampire nearly twelve hundred years ago. Except, no one told him he'd fall in love with a demon one day and spend eternity living in hell.

Jonathan and his clan are enjoying some much-needed time off after dealing with their demon problems. It's Jonathan's bad luck he accidentally sees inside Baptiste's head during a visit. Now they're —once again—pulled into the drama of demons as they try to help Baptiste. But Baptiste doesn't need rescuing. In fact, he holds the key to saving them.

1

Jonathan was adorable to watch. Seriously, Lire never needed to leave the house to stay charged at full power. Being a lilin demon, he fed on desire. Lust thrummed through their home. Jonathan was the center of it more often than not. While at the kitchen counter, in full Nephilim mode, Jonathan shook his ass to the music blasting from earbuds. His wings framed his ass perfectly, making for an adorable picture. He liked watching Jonathan. For demons, power was hypnotic—like a snake with a charmer controlling it. There were times when Lire was called to act as Goddess Celeste's personal guard. Before Jonathan, Lire hadn't encountered anyone more powerful than the goddess most called their god. But Jonathan was the typical Nephilim, even though they weren't common. Celeste was his grandmother. As Nephilims do, he'd surpassed his kin's power. It was a lucky thing for the world that Jonathan was good to his core. Otherwise, he could snuff out the planet with the snap of his fingers. Lire wasn't sure if Jonathan realized that yet. If he had, the knowledge hadn't corrupted him. Either way, Lire reveled in his presence, soaking up his power. It didn't hurt that Jonathan was easy on the eyes. Not that it mattered. No one touched his heart beyond his blood mates, Dougal and Faolan. They slept. Lire never did. That was why he sat, watching Jonathan shake his ass in the kitchen. Someone like Lire should never be left alone with his thoughts. His choosing to be good didn't change the fact that he was a demon. A seed of evil would always fester inside him.

Jonathan turned, catching sight of Lire. Instead of blushing, as most people caught dancing in their underwear would, Jonathan winked. He carried his coffee to the table and pressed a kiss to Lire's cheek before claiming a seat. That was another reason Jonathan was one of Lire's favorite people. He never saw a demon when he looked at Lire. It was like being reborn as something new.

"Good morning, cutie. Or evening. Whatever the fuck time it is," Jonathan said with a laugh. Jonathan was the only person in the house who could touch him without consequences. Too bad the man already had his blood mates before they'd met. Otherwise, Lire might have tried to change fate for him. He'd never thought to have a mate at all. Much less one he could freely touch.

"Hey, sexy. You're in a good mood."

"Of course I am," Jonathan said, draping his earbuds over his shoulders. His wings engulfed him as he sat. "I have all you gorgeous creatures under one roof. No one has tried killing me in a while. Everyone is smiling. I'm not looking a gift horse in the mouth."

Lire hated to point out the obvious. "Isn't inviting Baptiste over today doing just that? He wasn't thrilled to learn of my existence."

It was true. Baptiste and his pack hadn't loved the idea of Jonathan keeping a demon as part of his clan. The fact that Lire was one of Celeste's personal guards had gone a long way at soothing things, but old prejudices ran deep. The New Orleans faction had stayed away since learning Lire lived there.

Jonathan's smile dimmed a hair. "I've been thinking."

"You mean overthinking," Lire said, interrupting.

"Yes, but that's what makes me good at

investigation." That was true. Being an amazing investigative reporter was how the man came to be part of the Scottish clan of vampires. His curiosity had him digging and prying until he'd uncovered an entire world he hadn't known existed. Now he was their king.

"What brilliant thing have you churned out of that amazing brain now?" Lire knew he was laying it on thick. Jonathan was worth it. He wanted the carefree smile back.

Jonathan winked, proving he saw through Lire's game. "Don't you think it's odd that we searched for several months in countless areas for demons using the ports, yet Baptiste found one within five minutes after I asked?"

The clan was coming off months of searching for a pack of demons responsible for the disappearance of several young women. The vampires hadn't had much luck finding the pack on their own. That is, until Jonathan's blood mate Cin had been kidnapped. Somehow, Baptiste had magically found a demon to question within minutes of Cin's disappearance. Lire had thought it strange. As a pure demon—the seventh son of Asmodeus—Lire could easily find which ports the demons used to hunt for goods and people. He could smell his kind. Baptiste, on the other hand, shouldn't have had such an easy time of it. The leader of the New Orleans vampires was no more than a vampire himself, his powers limited as such.

"Are you thinking he had prior knowledge of the demons' dealings and chose to look the other way?"

Jonathan chewed on his bottom lip and stared at some point over Lire's shoulder, as if thinking things over. Finally, his gold gaze found Lire's once more. "I hate to suspect our new allies of anything untoward, but I won't risk our safety by turning a blind eye. Everything I love is under this roof."

Lire nodded. He understood. Everything he loved was under this roof as well. A smile that felt evil even to him stretched his lips. "How brazen would you like me to be in the inspection of his mind?"

Jonathan's expression turned wicked. "Good cop, bad cop?"

"I like the way your brain works." As the claim left his lips, the stirring of one of his mates scratched at his mind. Lire glanced over his shoulder, seeing only the images moving through his thoughts. Faol was awake. Lire's body stirred to life, itching to merge with another piece of his soul. Without thought, his body turned to smoke.

"Later," Jonathan said, his voice heavy with laughter and cutting through his focus.

Lire couldn't find any guilt in his heart for rushing away. The call of his blood mate was too strong. Lire concentrated on Faolan's location. His ginger warrior was in the shower. Lire closed his eyes and focused on joining with Faolan's body, becoming one. Faolan didn't fight him. Sometimes, he wondered if Faolan even noticed any longer unless he made himself known. Hot water streamed down Faolan's body. Lire felt the sensation as if it happened to him. Steam filled the bathroom. Lire used Faolan's hand to caress his skin. Along with Faolan, Lire's lust grew. Goddess Celeste had blessed him with two incredibly sexy mates. Lire loved touching Faolan. Unfortunately, being a full-blooded lilin demon meant he couldn't touch Faolan with his hands. Merging with Faolan was all he'd ever have of his mate.

What are you doing?

Faolan didn't sound irritated, merely curious.

I think we should play. Lire separated from Faolan's body but didn't solidify. Their thoughts were still one. *Keep your eyes closed. I promise you'll feel me.*

Ever the dutiful blood mate, Faolan closed his

eyes. His cheeks were already flushed. His large cock stood ready for anything. Lire kissed him. It was a simple brush of lips on lips. Being bodiless limited what Lire could do. He might not be capable of kissing Faolan the way he wanted, but he could make the man burn. Faolan's gasp proved he'd felt the light contact. Lire focused on their mental connection, touching Faolan's with his incorporeal fingertips while sending the image to Faolan's mind. Faolan's lips parted. His flush deepened. Lire stroked the man's stomach before slipping lower. Pre-cum rolled down Faolan's length. An ache grew in Lire's chest. He wanted to taste Faolan. It would never happen. Lire could possess Faolan because they'd never touched any way other than mentally. Lire wasn't just any sex demon, but the son of Asmodeus, the seventh prince of Hell—Lust. Lire was lust in its purest form. Direct contact with his skin could drive a man mad even if he was immortal like Faolan. Their blood mate, Dougal, had already touched Lire too many times. Lire couldn't possess him without making him insane. So, touching Faolan, even while using Dougal's body, was off limits. Their arrangement wasn't perfect, but it was all Lire had. All that he lived for. But as he watched Faolan's dick leak, Lire felt his isolation harder than usual. He loved men he could never touch with his hands or taste with his tongue. It was hell. He was a demon. Lire supposed he was exactly where he was meant to be.

He encircled Faolan's cock with his fingers and sent the image to Faolan. Faolan slapped his hand against the shower wall, holding himself up as he rocked against Lire's touch. Lire drew a deep breath through his nose. He fed from the lust coating the air. Like Faolan needed to drink blood to survive, Lire needed sex. The shower was filled with Faolan's desire. Lire became the glutton. He toyed with Faolan's balls. Played with his asshole. He milked the giant vampire's dick and massaged his prostate. Lire stared at his hands. He knew they weren't really there, but he never let that thought touch Faolan's mind. His love would only know pleasure.

"That's it, sexy. Fuck my fist. You make my dick so hard. I'd love to bend you over right now."

A pained-sounding moan bounced off the walls as Faolan drew closer to the edge. Lire could feel what he felt. Their minds were connected. Faolan's pleasure was his. Lire stroked faster. The sound of Faolan's dick pumping inside his fist only added to Lire's madness. He needed the man's release. Faolan tensed. For a moment, they were completely connected in every way as Faolan balanced on the edge of lust's blade. With a gasp, Faolan orgasmed. His hot cum passed through Lire's molecules, hitting the shower floor. Lire closed his eyes and fought for air as the distance between them disappeared.

His energy melded with Faolan's as he pictured himself holding Faolan. "I would give anything." He didn't need to finish his thoughts. Faolan's were the same. They would never touch in reality.

"I know," Faolan whispered, sounding every bit as broken.

Lire melted into Faolan, reclaiming his spot inside the man's body and becoming one. This was the most they'd ever have. In truth, it was closer than anyone else ever got, but they knew what they were missing.

I love you, demon.

Lire smothered his slight discontent. *I love you too, my fool. Why is our blond beauty still sleeping?*

A chuckle rang through Faolan's mind, making Lire quiver and forget his earlier unhappiness. *We wore him out.*

We should give him a treat for being such a put-upon mate.

Faolan killed the water in the shower and

headed for the bedroom without bothering to dry his skin. *I agree.*

Dougal was on his stomach with the sheet only covering his ass, and his head buried beneath a pillow. The rest of his gorgeous body was bare for the eye fucking. Faolan kissed the back of the man's thigh at the edge of the sheet. After shoving the material aside, he dragged his fangs up the man's ass. A moan sounded from beneath the pillow. Dougal rolled over. Gorgeous blue eyes peeked open. His long blond hair was a tangled mess around his face. Lire's pride mixed with Faolan's. Somehow, Goddess Celeste had chosen them to be this amazing man's mate. For eternity. Some people needed a sunset to remind them of how small they were in the universe. All Lire needed to do was look at his life. No other demon was as blessed.

"You don't believe in letting a man rest." The laughter in Dougal's voice let Lire know he didn't mean it.

Faolan licked his hip bone. "You can sleep all you want... later." He swirled his tongue around Dougal's navel. Damn, the man was beautiful. Lire no longer knew which of them wanted Dougal more, Faolan or him. Their emotions swirled together. "I love you."

Faolan's voice came out sounding demonic, since they'd both spoken at the same time.

"The feeling is so mutual," Dougal said, burying his hand in Faolan's hair.

Salty pre-cum coated his tongue. Lire settled in, letting Faolan do his thing and enjoying the ride along. Every sensation was his. As Dougal's hips lifted, openly fucking Faolan's mouth, the pride was his. He was a glutton among so much desire. He knew the moment would soon pass, and he'd have to let his men be, but for now, he soaked in their combined adoration. Lire refused to let his earlier discontent touch him here.

2

For the most part, Baptiste's Voodoo shop ran itself. Being in the heart of the French Quarter helped. People came to New Orleans looking to escape, whether it be through alcohol or a spell. Baptiste only served up one of those things. Most of the items lining the shelves were harmless. He had one or two regular customers who needed the real thing. Occasionally, he caught glimpses of people's worries, and he ensured they left with the right poppet for protection. After all, monsters were real. So too was Baptiste's magic. No one needed to know that beyond his vampire brethren—Ethan, Evan, and Dante. Dante had been his friend for more years than Baptiste could count, while the twins, Ethan and Evan, had only been around since Baptiste lost his mates three years ago.

He'd taken the men into his home, and he depended on them more than they'd ever know.

With Ethan and Evan's help, the shop didn't require his presence to keep running, but sometimes Baptiste liked sitting among the positive vibes while soaking up the hope of humans. No such emotion came to him organically any longer. A gorgeous blond Scotsman, wearing a kilt, drew more than one admiring glance as he cleared the doorway. Baptiste eyed the man for another reason. He was no man. If anyone looked closely enough, they'd spot the iridescent glow to his eyes. Most people's gazes never went that high when admiring the vampire king's personal guard. His body screamed hard labor and demanded lingering stares. He moved like a predator. The deadly vampire had killed many, many people in his years on earth. The Druid in Baptiste could hear their screams. Still, Baptiste was glad for the man's presence. His race needed strong men. After all, the enemy knew no mercy. Dougal's presence could only mean one thing—he'd been summoned by the king.

Baptiste circled the counter and met the guard halfway. He pasted on a smile. "Dougal. It's been a while."

Dougal dipped his chin. "Baptiste." The man's

eyes and hard features caught the light. Baptiste found himself staring. Dougal truly was magnificent. Baptiste had heard rumors of the past king of Scotland's fascination with Dougal. In Dougal's presence, Baptiste believed them all. "Jonathan has sent me to ask, if you're free, if you'd come for a visit."

"Have things been too quiet for him?" Baptiste laughed at his own inquiry to hide his discomfort.

The guard smirked. Baptiste stifled a sigh. Dougal was damn beautiful. "We are verra unaccustomed to sitting still, it's true. I believe this is no more than a social call. Jonathan isn't one..." Dougal stared into space for a second. He blinked, and a chuckle escaped him. "I started to say Jonathan isn't one to look for trouble, but the opposite is true. Not only does he often go looking, he tends to always find it."

Despite his bad humor today, Baptiste found himself smiling. He could picture Jonathan being just as Dougal described. "How can I resist that offer?" He cast a look at the bright sun still shining outside the shop. "There's no way you dissipated this early in the day." He couldn't. The sun dampened a vampire's powers.

"I took the bus," Dougal said, surprising a

chuckle from Baptiste. He couldn't imagine the looks he must've gotten.

Baptiste waved for Dougal to follow him to the back of the shop. "We'll take my car." Baptiste was hyper aware of the giant guard behind him. It wasn't that he expected an attack, or maybe he did. Baptiste had been walking on his toes for so long, he no longer knew who his friends were. His black Tahoe sat in the shade, saving them somewhat from the heat. It took a minute for the fifteen-year-old SUV to cool down, even with the air on full blast.

"Sorry," Baptiste said, trying to fill the silence. "I don't drive often enough to worry over getting a newer car."

"I do nay drive at all." Dougal kept his gaze locked ahead as he made the claim, doing nothing to alleviate Baptiste's discomfort.

"You should learn. It could save your life someday."

Dougal glanced over. His expression was clear of all emotion. "I know how. I just don't. At least, not here. It's too crowded for my blood."

"Oh." Baptiste sifted through his thoughts, doing his damnedest to think of something to say as he drove. "How are you liking it here?"

"It's hot," Dougal said, doing nothing to help move their conversation along.

"I'm sorry."

Dougal's tone never wavered from bland. "You apologize a lot."

"Sorry." Baptiste bit his bottom lip. "I'm socially inept," he confessed, hoping to make things better.

"I can tell." At Dougal's response, Baptiste decided to hold his tongue. Dougal obviously didn't care to talk, and Baptiste wasn't good at it, so he let it go. The king didn't live that far. Conversation was unnecessary. "There's nay wrong with being odd," Dougal said, finally breaking the silence. "My mate Faolan is a clown. Sometimes, he's a lot to handle."

Baptiste turned the image of the large ginger with amethyst eyes over in his head. He couldn't picture such a man being a jokester, but his mate would know. Before he knew it would happen, and with his gaze locked on the road, Baptiste found himself talking about something he never did. "My mate, Eirik, he was very much at odds with his appearance too. He was a Viking. A real one. His body was covered from head to foot in tattoos and deep scars from back when he was human. Back when such things were as painful as possible. When he looked at people, they would shy away because he looked mean." A smile touched Baptiste's lips. He could see Eirik as clear as he had the day they'd met. Piercing gray eyes. Long, blond braid hanging over one shoulder. "Then he'd open his mouth and floor you with how soft spoken he was."

"Do you wish to be with him in the afterlife, rather than being here?" Dougal asked, pulling Baptiste from his memories.

There was no condemnation in Dougal's question. It was obviously a feeling the man understood. Baptiste rubbed his chest. "Every day."

"It seems like I recall hearing something about him being a leader around here."

Baptiste nodded. "He was hard but fair, so people came to him when they had a problem, hoping he'd intervene on their behalf. When he passed, people started coming to me instead. It sort of stuck. That's the only reason I ended up being the new leader around here. Otherwise..." Baptiste waved toward himself and flashed Dougal a smile. "Awkward."

Dougal's laughter eased some of the tightness in Baptiste's chest. The tension left the air. The king's house came into view. The large ranch-style home was surrounded by trees, closing them off from the rest of the world. It also made it easy for Jonathan's guards to detect any intruders in time to protect their king. Baptiste's comfort lasted for as long as it took him to get inside. Faolan and Jonathan sat at the kitchen table with Lire, the demon. The tiny hairs on the back of Baptiste's neck stood. The king's tolerance for demons wasn't a feeling Baptiste shared. This one was powerful. It didn't matter that Celeste trusted him. Baptiste never would. He knew firsthand the damage they could cause.

Jonathan stood and met Baptiste halfway. "Hi. I'm so glad you had time for us," Jonathan said, shaking Baptiste's hand and leading him to the table. Dougal plopped down in the chair Jonathan had vacated between Lire and Faolan. Lire evaporated, becoming one with Faolan just long enough to kiss Dougal before reappearing where he'd been seated. Jonathan pulled out a chair across from Dougal, leaving Baptiste no other choice but to sit. He couldn't tear his eyes away from the demon and his mates. When Eirik had been alive, Baptiste had been in the same position as the three people sitting across from him. A triad of two vampires and a demon. It had been a mistake. Demons destroyed everything from the inside out, even matings.

"Would you like some coffee?"

"Um." Baptiste had nothing. His mind wouldn't budge from the three.

"You'll have coffee," Jonathan said, moving to the counter and pouring Baptiste a cup. He came back, holding out the mug for Baptiste to take.

"Where are your mates?" Baptiste asked Jonathan, making conversation as he accepted the cup. The need to stare at the demon in the room tore at his skin. He didn't like this. If he'd known the demon would be here, Baptiste wouldn't have come.

Jonathan smiled. His dimples showed, giving Baptiste something else to focus on. "Scotland. Niall's brother has taken over as king there. Cin and Niall are participating in their yearly games. Sort of a diplomatic mission."

Despite everything, a smile touched Baptiste's lips. "They're playing."

At Baptiste's observation, Jonathan's smile grew. His eyes, which already resembled a pot of leprechaun's gold, shimmered even brighter. "Yes. They're playing. These poor guys," he said, waving at the two vamps and one beast at the table, "got screwed. They're stuck guarding me."

"Nay," Dougal and Faolan said at the same time. It was Dougal who elaborated. "I have no wish ever to return to that place."

Baptiste couldn't imagine leaving New Orleans and never setting foot there again. Much less never wanting to return. Curiosity ate at him. He wondered if the rumors he'd heard about Dougal and Niall's father were why the men didn't wish to return to Scotland. It wasn't his business. Baptiste blinked several times, trying his ass off to keep his thoughts to himself. His mouth won. "I don't know how to change the topic to something less intrusive." A nervous laugh escaped him. "Sorry. I'm socially awkward." Like they hadn't noticed. His smile felt more like a grimace. "That's why I rarely visit," he tacked on, because no one was responding, and he couldn't stop trying to fill the silence. Still, no one spoke. Baptiste's shoulders fell. It seemed the comfort he'd found in the car, talking to Dougal, was gone. He rubbed his arms. In the privacy of his home and shop, Baptiste was free to be the functioning demon addict. Here, with a demon and his king watching, Baptiste barely stopped himself from flipping out. He massaged his left hand. He could feel everyone's eyes upon him, burning into his skin. Baptiste's gaze shot around the room, avoiding eye contact. He hated when the comfort of the norm evaded him. Baptiste couldn't stop the overwhelming feelings engulfing him.

"How long has it been since your mate died?"

Baptiste's gaze dropped to his chest. That was

how certain he was he'd been stabbed in the heart at Lire's question. The pain never lessened. He rubbed his arms again. The feeling of being exposed grew. "What?"

Lire waved a dismissive hand in his direction. "Only losing a mate causes the type of distress you're constantly in. How long has it been?"

A wave of unadulterated fury rose inside Baptiste. The demon spoke of things he didn't understand. Baptiste wanted to rip his throat out. His voice came out sounding as hard as Baptiste's face felt. "You're a mystery to me," Baptiste said instead of answering. "Why are you here?" He was incapable of not poking the demon even though it was so much worse than poking a bear. "Sometimes, you're here in body. Other times, you're here in spirit. Either way, you're always here, muddying the waters with your evil."

"He is our blood mate," Dougal growled, motioning between Faolan and himself, and transforming from the clan beauty to deadly warrior in an instant, all illusions of friendship gone. The man came to his feet, already reaching for his blade. His fangs bared, ready to defend his mate, as he should. Baptiste didn't doubt for a second the giant vampire felt his rage. He also couldn't pretend there wasn't a small part of him that hoped Dougal would strike, taking away Baptiste's never-ending pain.

Jonathan brushed his fingers down Dougal's back, and the man melted back into his seat.

Baptiste went on alert. He was a guest here and pissing off the king's guard shouldn't be on his to-do list. Before Baptiste could apologize, Lire slammed into Baptiste's mind. As clear as if it was happening, Baptiste saw himself nude—ass up and face pressed into his mattress. Lire's hard body weighed down on him.

"I can be as solid as I please," Lire whispered, sounding deadly as his dick stretched Baptiste's asshole wide without mercy inside his head. Like that, Baptiste was hard, panting, and on the edge of orgasm. The image of Lire transformed, becoming smoke. Baptiste's body absorbed him like water. It was as if Lire wore his skin. His limbs became Lire's. His thoughts, Lire invaded them all. None of it was real, but Baptiste couldn't tell the difference any longer. "Or I can be as incorporeal as I want. I can be a part of you, controlling you, and ensuring you feel every passion I desire. You would beg to do my bidding." Baptiste forcefully shoved Lire from his mind. The images disappeared, leaving Baptiste light-headed and off balance as he stared at Lire across the table from him. Lire looked intrigued by Baptiste's ability to take back control of his mind. Still, even though Lire had never moved, he'd made his point, and mentally wrecked Baptiste. "But, you already knew what I could do. Didn't you, Baptiste?"

Fucking demons. They were all the same. Possibly the king thought he had this one housebroken, but it wasn't true. Demons couldn't be tamed. They leveled everything. It was only a matter of time before the one sitting across from Baptiste brought down this entire household. Baptiste wasn't fooled by his act.

Spite rose inside Baptiste, taking control of his mouth. "Don't you want to know how I did it? Aren't you curious why you can't see who it is? How I'm stopping you from taking complete control of my mind?"

Everyone looked between Lire and Baptiste with open curiosity. As if watching a tennis match, waiting to see who'd win. There was no way they could know what had gone on mentally between them. No doubt, their conversation seemed odd to everyone else.

Baptiste didn't let up. He pulled his necklace up and over his head before holding it out to Dougal. "I expect this back." He enunciated every word, leaving no doubt he'd kill to retrieve the item. "Put it on."

Dougal glanced Lire's way. When Lire dipped his chin, Dougal accepted the necklace. He pulled it over his head. His eyebrows rose in question.

Baptiste switched his attention Lire's way. He motioned toward Dougal. "You should kiss your man. I imagine it's been a while since you've done so with your own lips."

Dougal's expression turned panicked. His gaze swung between them. "I'm not—"

Lire kissed him. They were both stiff, as if expecting the worse. Dougal was the first to melt. He touched Lire's face. Baptiste thought he'd feel smug and triumphant when Lire realized Baptiste held all the answers to freeing him from using one mate to touch the other. Instead, he just felt petty and empty. They were all equally at the mercy of cruel circumstance. When Lire tore his mouth away and stormed from the room, Baptiste's self-hatred doubled. Dougal's expression was devastated as he watched Lire disappear. Baptiste tried looking anywhere but at the man he'd hurt for no other reason than pettiness. Because he needed them down in the dirt where he lived. His gaze landed on Jonathan.

Jonathan's golden eyes stared a hole through Baptiste. *I see you.* His king's words rang through his mind like hot coals. *I see all of you.*

"You take this one," Jonathan said to Faolan unnecessarily, since the man was already rubbing Dougal's back. "I've got Lire," he added, following Lire from the room.

Faolan tugged Dougal into his arms, wrapping him in his embrace and comforting his mate. Baptiste couldn't look away. He saw nothing. Misery truly did love company, but he didn't feel better about himself for dragging the throuple down to his level. Instead, he realized how loving Kallus had corrupted his soul.

Dougal kept his gaze averted as he handed Baptiste's necklace back. "Thank you."

Baptiste had never felt crueler because—just as Jonathan did—he knew the truth. Baptiste hadn't meant to give Dougal and Lire a kiss without the madness of touching the spawn of pure lust. Baptiste had meant to punish Lire with what he could never have. He saw too much of himself in this situation. Baptiste couldn't stay silent.

He focused on the amethyst-eyed vampire who'd kept his silence. "You should expel him. Send the demon away before he destroys you."

All gratitude fled from Dougal. "It's past time you should leave. You insult us."

Baptiste didn't back down or look away from Faolan. "What do you think will happen if this one dies?" he asked, motioning toward Dougal. "I'll tell you what will happen, because it happened to me when Eirik died. Your demon can't touch you. The only thing holding you together is your blond beauty. If he goes, do you think your demon will stay? He won't," Baptiste answered without giving Faolan time to respond. "Having two mates is a blessing straight from Goddess Celeste. Losing one is a nightmare you can never escape. Losing two." Baptiste shook his head. "There's no description excruciating enough. You should expel him. Cling to what's real." Baptiste stood, his welcome gone. "Expel him," Baptiste repeated before heading for the door. He didn't need to hear Faolan's agreement. It was in the man's eyes. He knew Baptiste was right. He was the disposable mate. Just as Baptiste had been.

Lire hovered in the air like smoke. He had nowhere to go. Jonathan wouldn't let him get away even if he did. Jonathan knew the demon also couldn't join with Faolan right now. Not if he didn't want Faolan to hear all the thoughts Jonathan didn't have the luxury of shutting out. Lire's mind was a mess, but he wasn't the type to let his mates think for a second he was unhappy with their deal. Jonathan strode through the room. His steps never faltered as he headed Lire's way. Before the demon could disappear, Jonathan's arms encircled Lire, forcing his body to solidify. Jonathan's wings engulfed them, creating a cocoon no one could breach. With Jonathan's forehead pressed to his, Lire's gaze showed his pain. Nothing escaped Jonathan. He showed Lire no pity. He knew Lire was one kind word away from losing his shit.

Instead, Jonathan handed him the hard truth. "That man is in there; he's telling your mates to abandon and expel you. He's saying you'll leave. That they don't matter."

Lire's expression turned pained in a way Jonathan had never seen. "I can never touch them. Being with them seemed like such a blessing, but I'm more isolated than ever." Lire whispered every word, baring his darkest secrets to Jonathan, even though Jonathan already knew. "I'm failing my mates, because I hate this. You can never tell. Promise me."

Jonathan nodded. His gaze never wavered. "Do you trust me?"

"I do," Lire said without hesitation.

"We're about to make a deal. After I do something for you, you'll do something for me, and you'll trust me every step of the way."

"Everything I have is yours." Lire meant it. Jonathan heard it in his voice. Jonathan knew Lire would follow him above all others. It was there, showing at the forefront of Lire's thoughts.

"Call your mates." Jonathan could do it, but he needed Lire grounded. At his demand, Dougal and Faolan appeared. They didn't bother walking. The men appeared from thin air, looking ready to battle.

A smile that felt overly bright, even to Jonathan, stretched Jonathan's lips. "I didn't mean for you to be quite so intense about it, but we're all here now. Turn around."

Lire turned without question, facing his men. Jonathan's arms encircled him from behind. Lire's overheated skin warmed Jonathan's chest. Jonathan's skin glowed like the sun, making Jonathan want to close his eyes against the sight. He still hadn't gotten used to odd things happening to his body since growing into his Nephilim powers. This was one time he couldn't pretend it wasn't happening. He needed all his strength.

Jonathan felt Lire's intensity dampen as he soaked in the unnatural lust Lire bled nonstop.

"Do you trust me?" Jonathan asked again, this time posing the question to Dougal and Faolan.

"With our lives," they both repeated in unison.

Jonathan's throat tightened with love for his clan. What he was about to demand of them meant they'd be risking everything if he failed. Jonathan wouldn't let them down. "This is all that I can give you, but unlike Baptiste, I don't do this with spite in my heart. Faolan, kiss your mate."

Faolan's eyebrows rose. He didn't budge.

"Do you believe in me?" Jonathan asked, feeling a bit desperate. He couldn't hold Lire's powers at bay forever.

Faolan squared his shoulders. "Aye."

"Then kiss him before you miss your chance."

The distance between them disappeared. Faolan's mouth covered Lire's. Love exploded through the room. The desire coating Lire's skin doubled, nearly bringing Jonathan to his knees. He panted against the assault, but he wasn't done. "Dougal, it's now or never."

Dougal's longing joined the mixture of emotions

crushing Jonathan's brain as Dougal joined their kiss without Faolan's hesitation. Jonathan pressed his forehead to Lire's nape, squeezed his eyes shut, and tried hanging on.

Thank you. Lire's words caressed Jonathan's mind as he disentangled himself from his loves, as if he felt Jonathan weakening. The moment they were no longer touching, Jonathan sprang away. His chest heaved with every labored breath. With his hands braced on his knees, Jonathan sucked air. Jonathan was bursting at the seams with madness and desire. He was part god and Lire's powers were consuming him. For the first time, Jonathan understood the full magnitude of what Dougal endured when he'd lived with Lire before their mating. It was no wonder the vampire had been willing to walk into the fire, choosing a warrior's death over the idea of never having Lire again.

Niall and Cin appeared. Cin had guns drawn, searching for a threat. Niall held a giant claymore. Under different circumstances, Jonathan might have found that funny. Right now, with Lire's powers breaking his mind, Jonathan couldn't focus on anything but the insanity.

"What the fook is happening here?" Niall demanded, looking thunderous.

Jonathan tried answering, but his throat refused to work. His mates stood feet away. Jonathan fought the urge to rip into their skin to be an inch closer to them. His body burned. He needed relief. With a mere thought, Jonathan had them in their bed unclothed. He didn't often use his gifts against Niall and Cin. After willingly exposing himself to lilin corruption, Jonathan needed the madness assuaged now, or he might do anything.

"Are you okay?"

Jonathan had never heard Niall sound so worried. "Fix me." The growl in Jonathan's voice was out of his control.

Cin kissed his neck, making Jonathan writhe and his dick leak. "We've got you, gorgeous. Niall and I will make you fly," he promised.

Jonathan's legs wouldn't still. He ground them against the sheets, needing contact with reality.

Niall bit his shoulder as he rolled Jonathan onto his side. His large crown pressed against Jonathan's asshole even as Cin's hot mouth surrounded Jonathan's cock. Jonathan came unglued. He'd been barely hanging on from the moment he absorbed Lire's energy. Words left his lips. He had no idea what he said. Most likely, he begged for a hard fucking. Jonathan didn't want to limp away from this. He needed his men to destroy him. Take away the insanity. Cin sucked hard, tearing a cry from Jonathan's throat. Niall fucked him raw. The sound of skin slapping against skin filled the room. Jonathan came. His orgasm gave him no relief. Thankfully, Cin never paused. He drank Jonathan down, his tongue lapping away at Jonathan's hard dick. Every sensation was heightened. Jonathan felt every taste bud and breath on his cock. He needed more.

Jonathan tugged at Cin's hair, urging him away and up his body. He captured the man's mouth, licking his tongue and trying to taste his own cum. He nipped at Cin's lip and tasted blood. His fangs were at full glory. Like a shark in the water, his mate's blood threw Jonathan into a frenzy. The madness wouldn't subside.

"I want inside you. Let me inside." Even to Jonathan's ears, he sounded crazed. Neither Cin nor Niall hesitated to give Jonathan everything he needed. They shifted positions. With Cin's face down and ass up, Jonathan buried himself inside Cin, even as Niall fucked him. They'd gotten good at this. With his dick buried root deep in Cin's ass, Jonathan sank his fangs in the man's neck. His mate's blood filled his mouth, bringing the first ounce of sanity back to Jonathan. The pull on his cock felt more like pleasure and less like necessity. Then Niall bit him, stealing Jonathan's blood. The room steadied. His pace slowed.

Reaching over his head, Jonathan held Niall's dark hair, pushing back against him before sinking into Cin. He chose their pace, rocking slower with each pump of his hips. They were one. Connected in heart, body, and soul. These were the mates fate had chosen for him. He would've chosen them without help from the universe. Love replaced the insanity.

"Damn," Jonathan breathed, licking Cin's nape. "I love you both, so much. Two weeks is too long to be apart."

"Aye," Cin breathed.

"Agreed," Niall growled against his throat.

Niall's dick hit all the perfect spots. Cin's tight heat milked Jonathan's cock. The pleasure was too much. Jonathan reached for relief. Without warning, an orgasm slammed into him, stealing his breath. The room went dark as its intensity robbed him of sight.

Niall gasped. "Fook, Jonathan. That's it. I need that ass sucking on my cock."

Cin's orgasm washed over Jonathan's brain, combining with his. When Niall's pleasure filled his head too, Jonathan collapsed. His body couldn't contain the intensity of their ecstasy. Wave after wave of sexual satisfaction locked down his muscles, paralyzing him. Jonathan was trapped in its web. His back hit the mattress. Cin's and Niall's tongues filled his mouth. He reveled in how they entwined, taking turns savoring one another. Sweat and cum slickened their skin. The room smelled like sex and love. It was Jonathan's version of heaven. He wouldn't stop until Lire, Dougal, and Faolan had the same.

Lire, bring me Kallus. First born son of Mammon. Send Faolan to collect Baptiste at my command. Leave Dougal here to help me prepare a demon trap.

Anything, my king.

Baptiste might not think he cared about the mate who'd abandoned him, but as Jonathan snuggled in the cocoon of his mates, he knew better. There was no length he wouldn't go to protect his men. It was time to see if Baptiste would be the same.

3

With rage coating his brain and darkness streaking the sky, Baptiste skipped walking past the sea of knowing gazes and appeared inside his bedroom. Fuck all. The new king knew about Eirik and Kallus. He'd seen everything. Baptiste had felt the Nephilim penetrating his every thought and memory. Everything felt raw and exposed. No one understood the insanity. Baptiste tore up the floor, pacing from one end of the room to the other. Each time he closed his eyes, he saw Eirik's face—felt his mate's fangs piercing his skin. Then his eyes would open and Eirik would be gone, forever isolated from Baptiste, even in the next life. As a Viking, Eirik would rest in the halls of Valhalla. As a Druid, Baptiste would be reborn, over and over again until the end of time. That was why he'd chosen to turn vampire to begin with. At least as he was now, he'd been allowed to choose the form he would be forever. Forever had never seemed so unending. Without Eirik, he felt every drawn-out second as it ticked by. If their fates were different, Baptiste would've joined Eirik in the next life long ago.

Baptiste felt Kallus a half second before the demon's image filled his mind. Fingers encircled Baptiste's throat, gently urging him back against an unnaturally hot chest. Baptiste's eyes fell closed. In a detached way, Baptiste recognized Kallus wasn't really there. Everything was inside his head. The desperation he felt at Kallus' touch was all on him. It was the ghosts of his memories. The demon's greed couldn't touch him like this, but he could invade Baptiste's mind and drive him insane.

Baptiste hissed as Kallus brushed his lips across the shell of his ear. His knees weakened. As always, with just one touch, Kallus owned him. "I've been waiting for you to come home. You know I'm not a patient man."

"You're not a man at all," Baptiste argued, because it was better than begging.

Kallus ignored him. "Where have you been? I couldn't see you where you went." He pressed his nose to Baptiste's neck and inhaled. "You smell like power." Kallus hummed. "Damn. You know how much I love that scent."

Fuck. Baptiste hated him. Not as much as he hated himself, but still. Baptiste hardened his heart against Kallus and stepped out of the demon's hold. When he turned and met Kallus' gorgeous blue gaze, Baptiste saw all the weakness inside himself. Kallus was beautiful. With his iridescent light blue eyes, tall frame, black hair, and perfect lips, Kallus could fill any heart with instant greed. Every time Baptiste set eyes on the demon, it was just like the first. His heart squeezed in his chest. Every heartbeat came faster than the last. His throat went dry, bringing about the deepest thirst. Except it wasn't water he craved. Baptiste wanted to drink in every ounce of Kallus, owning the man in ways no one else ever could. Each time he saw Kallus, he felt the same. The thing was—he already owned Kallus in a way no one else ever would. Kallus was his blood mate, and Baptiste meant nothing to him at all. These imaginary meetings were just one of Kallus' many tricks. He toyed with Baptiste's mind and heart.

"What do you want?"

Kallus smirked. "Everything. You used to love

that about me. Come on," Kallus said, moving in close. "Play with me, Little Mouse."

The pain in Baptiste's chest stole his breath. "Don't call me that." He couldn't hear the pet name Eirik and Kallus had used for him right now.

Kallus mimicked his Cajun accent. "My shy little mouse," he taunted, closing the final gap between them. "If people could only see the pervert living beneath the awkward shell, I'd have to fight men off with a stick."

"*Exorcizo te, omnis te mentiri dicas.*"

His demon's smile fell. "No."

Baptiste couldn't hear it. "*Exorcizo te, omnis immundus corde. Oro, audite me.*" The image of Kallus disappeared from Baptiste's head, leaving him disoriented. The exorcism took Kallus away, but not the greed and longing. Baptiste's body betrayed him. His knees nearly hit the floor.

Ethan burst through his bedroom door, guns drawn, and looking ready for battle. The usual smooth flirt vanished beneath the picture of a beast. Ethan's dark-blue gaze bounced around the room, searching for a threat. He holstered his weapons behind his back when he found Baptiste alone. His long stride ate up the distance between them. The man's solid form braced Baptiste against a fall. His strong arms engulfed Baptiste. Ethan was a Prampire —part of a rare vampire sect that fed on strong emotional energy. No one knew. Baptiste kept Ethan and his twin Evan's secret. In turn, Ethan kept Baptiste sane. Without Ethan, losing Eirik and Kallus would've killed him long ago. The anger, love, hate, and want shifted. Baptiste felt it seep from his body as Ethan absorbed the emotions until they were muted. He held on, shaking in his relief.

"I've got you," Ethan whispered against his temple.

Baptiste turned his head. Ethan lowered his chin. Their lips met. It meant nothing. Baptiste didn't want anything beyond the physical response of touching. Their tongues met and stroked. For Baptiste, there was no huge explosion of passion. There never would be. He was mated to the demon who'd abandoned him. As long as Kallus still lived, Baptiste would never feel a quarter of what he felt for his mate for anyone else. It was akin to living in hell. Everything in his life was an echo of a whisper without his mates. Ethan was better than Kallus. He'd be a true mate to Baptiste. All Kallus did was steal and take from Baptiste, leaving him hollow and without hope. Baptiste nipped at Ethan's bottom lip, wanting to feel anything. Ethan's moan vibrated through their kiss. The final inch between them disappeared as Ethan shuffled closer. His erection dug into Baptiste's hip.

It didn't matter Baptiste's emotions were dampened. He could make Ethan fly. His fingers shaped Ethan's hard cock through his jeans. Ethan deepened their kiss. Baptiste went for the man's zipper, determined to make the man feel everything he couldn't. He could feel enough for this. A knock landed on his bedroom door, freezing them.

Evan's voice came through the door. "You have a visitor."

Baptiste bit back a growl. "I'll be there in a minute." Without a qualm, he set Ethan's erection free. The silky-smooth skin of a hard dick brushed his palm. "I can show my appreciation in record time."

Ethan pushed his hand away. He zipped his pants. With his gaze locked on his task, Ethan headed for the door. "I'm not interested in a pity hand job."

A growl choked Baptiste. "That's not what I meant."

"You have a visitor," Ethan reminded him. He was out the door before Baptiste could respond.

While scrubbing his hands through his hair,

Baptiste stared at the ceiling, seeking answers from above. Why? Why had he been left with this? Just why? Baptiste wasn't a warrior or a politician. Yet, people came to him, seeking answers and help. In truth, Baptiste had always been a lover and a scholar. All he cared to have was a book and someone to hold. He liked quiet and wine. Why had he been handed a life so at odds with him? He didn't know how to fight this battle.

"You should've let me die, Eirik. If you'd lived and let me die, my soul would've found you in the next life. Now, I am nothing. Without hope."

"Do you talk to yourself a lot?"

Baptiste dropped his chin as a thick Scottish accent filled his bedroom. "I wasn't talking to myself. It's rude to enter a man's bedroom without an invitation."

Faolan's amethyst eyes flashed with humor. "Considering how you left earlier, I didn't think you were too concerned with manners. If you're not talking to yourself, then who are you chatting with? You look to be quite alone to me."

"My blood mate, Eirik. I don't know if he hears me in the afterlife, but..." Baptiste shrugged. "Did you need something?"

With his shoulder leaned against Baptiste's door

frame, the man eyed him. His expression unreadable. "I was given to understand you have a second mate. One still living."

A snort escaped Baptiste. He moved to the bed and sat. His knees were still weak from Kallus' mind invasion and Ethan's kiss. "Having a blood bond with someone doesn't mean they'll stay. He abandoned me," Baptiste clarified.

"I'm verra sorry to hear that."

"He's a demon. They're not reliable." Baptiste didn't know why he couldn't shut up.

"Ah," Faolan said, straightening. "That explains the raging earlier. You do realize that not every demon is the same, right? Lire is quite steady. In fact, he's one of Goddess Celeste's personal guards. You should get to know someone before..." Faolan waved his hand, as if physically searching for the right term.

"Projecting my issues onto others," Baptiste supplied.

Faolan snapped his fingers and pointed at Baptiste. "That."

Baptiste blew out a tired-sounding breath. "I used to be so level-headed." A smile tugged at Baptiste's lips. "And then this rowdy bunch of Vikings blew through town. Damn," Baptiste said absently. "That feels like so long ago. Forever is a very long time."

Rather than running from Baptiste's maudlin mood, as most warriors would, Faolan moved closer. "You should come around more often. Being around Jonathan is like standing in the sunshine. Without all the nasty vamp damages, of course. He soothes the soul."

Baptiste flashed Faolan a sad smile. "I probably won't get many invites after today."

"Well, now, that's not true. I've been sent to fetch you back."

With a snort of laughter, Baptiste fell backward across the bed and stared at the ceiling. Would this day never end? "Am I being forced to apologize?" A horrible thought hit Baptiste. "Is Lire here too?"

A loud sigh rent the air. "My mate can be trying and pushy. He's not perfect, but he won't force you to hand him a shite apology you don't mean. Plus, knowing Lire as I do, I'm sure he wasn't innocent in your argument earlier. And, no, Lire isn't here. He's busy with our king. Jonathan has some reason all his own for sending me to fetch you."

Baptiste sat up. For now, Jonathan hadn't pushed his politics on the New Orleans sect since his arrival. The least Baptiste could do was continue working with him. "Can you give me a few minutes? I have some shit to work out here first."

Faolan nodded. "I'll wait in the kitchen."

Baptiste nodded and followed him from the room. When Faolan hit the stairs, Baptiste headed down the hall. Ethan's bedroom door was closed. Baptiste hesitated before finally deciding knocking would be best.

The door flew open, and a pissed-off-looking Ethan glared out at him. "What?"

Baptiste's chest hurt. He was failing everyone, including himself. "I'm being summoned back to our king."

Ethan's expression transformed from anger to concern in an instant. "Would you like me to guard your back?"

"Please?" Even though Baptiste trusted Jonathan, he didn't like feeling exposed as he had earlier in the day. He needed someone in his corner. Ethan never would've let Lire get to him. He would keep Baptiste safe.

Ethan nodded, becoming the amazing friend he'd always been. "Of course."

Baptiste swallowed hard. He wouldn't pretend nothing happened. Ethan's feelings mattered to him. "I'm sorry."

A line appeared between Ethan's eyes. His hardened expression made him twice as hot. Reaching out, he snagged the front of Baptiste's t-shirt and hauled him forward. His lips touched Baptiste's in a soft kiss. Baptiste breathed in the other man's scent. Their foreheads touched. Baptiste kept his eyes shut. He loved Ethan. It wasn't a passionate love. There was no jealousy or insanity as he'd sometimes felt with his mates. It was a peaceful and steady love filled with friendship. He trusted Ethan. Ethan would never hurt him. That was why it broke Baptiste that he was hurting Ethan.

"I know," Ethan whispered, taking away the guilt the way he always did. "Let's go find out why this king has suddenly taken such an interest in you."

Baptiste's heart sank. There was no time like the present to get this over with, but afterward, maybe he would go away. He'd been in New Orleans too long. There was nothing keeping him. Evan and Dante could run the shop. Once the thought set in, Baptiste felt lighter. He would leave. Eirik and Kallus were gone. It was well past time for him to move on to a new life too.

AFTER SQUARING HIS SHOULDERS, AND WITH DOUGAL guarding his back, Jonathan strolled inside the room they'd readied for Kallus. Jonathan wasn't prepared for the sight of the demon. When he'd met Lire, Lire had been ever-changing, keeping Jonathan on his toes. Kallus was solid and beautiful. Demons had to be breathtaking. That was how they stole souls and corrupted minds. Still, Jonathan hadn't been prepared. With jet black hair that begged to be touched and shimmering blue eyes, Kallus was heart-stoppingly perfect. Topping off those features, the demon's lips were amazing. They drew the eye. Having Kallus and Dougal in the same room was almost too much.

Kallus eyed them, his expression unreadable. "Damn. You are amazing," Kallus said, breaking the silence.

Jonathan glanced Dougal's way. "He is, isn't he? Unfortunately, for you, he's already mated."

A snort escaped Kallus. "I meant you," Kallus said, surprising Jonathan. "Blondie is hot, but you are... *mhmm.*" Kallus inhaled. "I recognize the scent of overwhelming power but can't recall where I've encountered it."

"*Och*, he's a smooth one, my king," Dougal said with a chuckle at Jonathan's back.

Jonathan claimed the empty chair outside Kallus' reach. "Demons usually are."

"King?" Kallus asked, sounding only mildly curious. "Ah," he said, before Jonathan could respond. "The new king of the Americas. I've heard the rumors." His heated gaze swept down Jonathan's body. "This is the first time I've met a Nephilim. Not that it matters. King. Nephilim. Grandson of Goddess Celeste. It matters not at all. You have no power over me. My father is a prince of hell. I answer only to the underworld."

The smile tugging at the corners of Jonathan's mouth was out of his control. Kallus wasn't unlikable. That was a good thing. He held up the book he'd brought with him. "Actually, this book says different. I'm new at this, so my brother-in-law Lachlan, who's the king of Scotland, dug up this book for me." He toyed with the ragged corners of the book that was bound in things Jonathan tried not to think about. It was old. "Who knew there was a book of rules and responsibilities for vampire kings? I certainly didn't." Jonathan flashed Kallus a smile. "Thank goodness I'm a nerd who loves to read, because riveting it is not. However, there are a few very interesting tidbits. Like, did you know demon and vampire matings aren't unheard of, as I expected. In fact, as uncommon as it might be, it's obviously happened enough to warrant a section in this book. It seems when you mated with Eirik and Baptiste, you became my problem."

"Oh, sexy, I'm everyone's problem," Kallus said with a wink. "More for some than others, but not everyone fights their demons. Some people prefer to spank them."

Jonathan held the man's stare until his smile fell and he shifted uncomfortably beneath Jonathan's gaze. Only when Jonathan was certain Kallus wouldn't continue saying stupid shit did he continue. "You abandoned your mate."

"Have you come to drag me home? Have you cleaned up all the world's problems to the point you resorted to trying your hand at marriage counseling now?"

Jonathan shook his head. "I'm only explaining your present circumstances. It's not in my nature to hold a prisoner without listing the charges. Since you're Mammon's son, I'm sure you don't care, but abandoning a mate is a serious offense. I'm assuming you knew the responsibility you undertook when you possessed Baptiste's body and used him to make the blood exchange with Eirik?"

Kallus wasn't smiling now. Pain radiated from the

man in waves. It took all Jonathan's self-control to keep a hard face. If he lost his mates, he would go with them. He couldn't imagine Kallus' position. "I knew," Kallus said so low Jonathan barely heard.

Jonathan nodded. "Then I have to assume you also knew it was against our laws to abandon your mate, since there's no such thing as divorce, and living apart can be unusually cruel."

"Yes." Kallus looked accepting.

"Very well," Jonathan said, coming to his feet. "I'll have Baptiste contacted. He'll decide your fate."

Kallus wiped his palms on his thighs and cleared his throat. He didn't look at Jonathan. "What are his options?"

Jonathan could see his thoughts. Kallus wasn't concerned for himself. He didn't want to hurt Baptiste any more than he already had. "If he says to send you on your way, I will. He might choose to leave you here until you starve or go mad." Kallus' gaze shot to Jonathan. Jonathan didn't hold back. "Or he has the option to have you destroyed, freeing him to move on."

Kallus gave him a short nod. Being the son of greed had him fighting his natural need to spread discord, but Jonathan felt the shift in his mind.

Kallus wanted to die, but he also wanted Baptiste to be the one to choose. "Okay."

Jonathan clasped his book to his chest. "While I have you here, I do have one question. Not too long ago, we had a visit from your father. He kidnapped one of my mates, hoping to force me to kill Baptiste."

Kallus' face hardened. He was still gorgeous, but it was a deadly beauty. "I did not send Mammon to kill my mate," Kallus growled.

Jonathan didn't miss the fact that he hadn't referred to Mammon as his father. "That wasn't my question. My question is—did he want Baptiste dead because of you?"

"Did you destroy him? Mammon, that is?"

"He left me no choice but to send him back to the underworld," Jonathan said without an ounce of guilt.

"Then the answer to your question is yes. Eirik is dead because of me, and he won't stop until Baptiste suffers the same fate."

It was as Jonathan suspected. Kallus had abandoned his mate to save him. The damage was the same, nonetheless. "That won't be happening on my watch. I'll send for Baptiste."

"You should've killed Mammon," Kallus called at

his back, sounding desperate. "Because he won't stop."

Jonathan opened the door and turned. "If we cross paths again, he won't walk away."

Dougal followed Jonathan from the room, protecting his back, even though they'd warded the place to the teeth. The moment the door was closed behind them, Dougal snagged Jonathan's arm, pulling him to a stop. Their gazes met. Unexpectedly, Dougal wrapped Jonathan in a tight hug. The man's emotions overwhelmed Jonathan, choking him and filling his eyes with tears. Dougal quickly stepped back. He cleared his throat and tapped his chest.

"I've never been prouder to serve anyone or call them my friend."

Jonathan blinked. Dougal wasn't an overly emotional person. His words meant the world to Jonathan, especially since he questioned his every decision, certain he was fucking up everything he touched. "Love you," Jonathan said, scurrying away before he looked like an idiot.

Faolan, bring him.

Now all he could do was wait and see if he deserved Dougal's loyalty.

4

This time, Baptiste didn't have to worry over awkwardness on his trip to Jonathan's. It was dark enough that their powers were heightened, and they dissipated, moving effortlessly from one place to the next in an instant. As Baptiste cleared the doorway of the king's home, he felt an odd pulse in the air. The sensation seemed familiar, but the memory stayed just out of his grasp. Jonathan and Dougal sat side by side at the kitchen table, drinking coffee and talking in quiet tones. They glanced up as Baptiste, Faolan, and Ethan came through the door.

Jonathan's smile was welcoming. "Hi. Sorry to drag you back after you stormed out with such amazing parting shots earlier."

Baptiste almost apologized. The words rose to

his lips. He bit them down. Lire had started it by pushing his way into Baptiste's mind. Hell would freeze before Baptiste regretted standing up for himself. He might be awkward, but he wasn't weak. Eirik never would've loved a weak man. "Why am I back?"

Jonathan's gaze shifted Ethan's way. He hesitated before nodding, as if coming to some internal decision. "Faolan, would you take Ethan on a tour of the house while I talk to Baptiste? I'm sure he would love to see our armory."

Ethan crossed his arms over his chest and planted his feet. "I'm not going anywhere. You allowed your demon to attack his mind earlier today. I won't allow it twice."

Jonathan's face hardened. Baptiste found the sight oddly fascinating. The king was such a nice person. The look didn't suit him. "That won't be happening again. However, I can see everything and everyone—feel what they feel. But you're different. Somehow, you're blocking me, which means you have something to hide. I can't trust a man who keeps secrets. Unless you're willing to tell us what you're hiding, you can go with Faolan."

"I'll hold you at your word about protecting Baptiste. Don't doubt that I have powers of my own."

Without meeting anyone's gaze, Ethan followed Faolan from the room. Baptiste's unease doubled. He'd asked Ethan to accompany him for a reason. Now he was left unprotected. It wasn't that he thought Jonathan or his clan would hurt him. Baptiste felt something in the air. Something benevolent. He wanted to run. Instead, he moved to the kitchen table and sat.

Once Jonathan had him isolated, his expression turned kind again. "I have Kallus."

Baptiste flew back to his feet, ready to bolt. Only his weakened knees stopped him from fleeing.

Jonathan raised his arms, making a calming gesture. "Please? Just sit and hear me out."

After several deep breaths, Baptiste managed to call his racing heart under control. Baptiste sat. He understood now the disarray of his thoughts. Kallus was here. Under the same roof. Breathing the same air. It was too much. Baptiste opened his mouth, intent on asking a thousand questions. No sound emerged. Everything hurt too badly. He couldn't function.

Jonathan nodded, as if he understood. "I know this is painful for you. That's exactly why this needs to be addressed. By mating with a vampire, Kallus now falls under my rule. He has to be judged and sentenced for abandoning his mate."

Baptiste found his voice. "I don't understand. It's been so long. Why do this now? It's like opening an old wound that won't heal properly."

"There hasn't been a king here for a very long time. Before now, he hasn't had anyone to answer to. Now he does. When you were here earlier, you showed Dougal a kindness by giving him a moment with Lire."

"That wasn't kindness," Baptiste spat. He couldn't get a handle on his emotions. They were flying in every direction.

Jonathan shook his head. "Whatever your reasons were, your gesture made me realize how much we could help one another."

Realization dawned. This wasn't about him at all. Jonathan wanted something from him. "Wait," he said, holding up his hand and stopping Jonathan from saying more. "Am I being blackmailed? Are you doing this, hoping I'll help Lire with his inability to touch his mates?"

Jonathan blinked, looking surprised by Baptiste's questions. "The fact that you would even ask that proves you don't know me at all. No. You're not being blackmailed. I got the impression earlier you could use some help. Celeste put me in this position for a reason because she knew I could do some good here. Go see him. Take back your life. Forever is a damn long time to have a mate who won't be one." He pushed to his feet, obviously intent on walking away before Baptiste could piss him off even more. "Dougal will go with you for your protection."

Baptiste stood too. "Point me in the right direction. I don't need protection. There's nothing Kallus could do to me that's worse than what he's already done."

The king's golden gaze swirled as he stared at Baptiste. His face set. "Still, Dougal will accompany you. He can stand outside the door, if it pleases you, but he's going." Without waiting for Baptiste to argue further, Jonathan walked away. Lire followed the king from the room, leaving Dougal behind.

Baptiste's gaze slid Dougal's way. "If this isn't blackmail, what is it?"

Dougal motioned toward the hallway. "Kindness. Follow me."

"It doesn't feel like kindness," Baptiste grumbled. A soft chuckle floated through the air. Baptiste bit back a growl at the sound. "I'm being serious. Kallus abandoned me years ago. I haven't set eyes on him since. This feels a lot like torture."

Dougal stopped outside a bolted door and focused on Baptiste. "Jonathan is unfailingly kind. He'd never intentionally hurt you. Take his advice and his gift. It's time to face this and move on. Or do you like living in limbo?"

Baptiste gave Dougal a sharp nod. He needed this over with. Dougal opened the door. Kallus stood in the center of the room. For a moment, Baptiste couldn't move. His feet froze to the floor. Then, he was across the threshold and the door closed behind him, shutting him away—alone with his mate for the first time in years. Baptiste had seen the visions of Kallus the demon sent him when he wanted to play, and he caught glimpses of his mate in his dreams, but there was nothing in heaven or on earth to compare to the real thing. He made men greedy. Those goddamn lips. People talked about looks coming from the devil. They had no idea. One glance Kallus' way could cripple a man with a gut-wrenching need for more. But the demon had been aptly named, because Kallus was cold and cruel, uncaring of the damage he caused. No one knew better than Baptiste. He was dressed to the nines—like they caught him at a goddamn movie premiere.

The room had nothing inside other than two straight-back chairs—one on each side of the wards.

It was more than obvious this was nothing more than an interrogation room. Kallus spoke first, sending chills down Baptiste's spine with the reminder of what only he could do for Baptiste.

"I hear the new king wants you to judge me?"

"You'd better hope not," Baptiste said, sounding detached even to his ears. He had to hold himself apart for his sanity. "For your sake, you'd better pray he decides to choose your punishment. I'll let you rot. Wherever you've been, it seems to have kept you well." Baptiste didn't bother sitting. He wouldn't be here that long. Plus, he would never give Kallus the advantage of hovering over him.

Kallus eyed him, raking Baptiste with a hot gaze from head to toe. "Damn. You're still the sexiest man alive. You should tell this so-called king to let me go. We have catching up to do."

Loathing boiled in Baptiste's veins. He wanted blood. Baptiste craved the sight of Kallus' acidic blood coating the walls, but more than that, he wanted the man to suffer. Long and hard. "Let's catch up now," Baptiste said, moving closer.

Kallus took a step back. His bravado fled. "You can't touch me. You don't want that."

Dark emotions brewed in Baptiste, driving him on. He kept moving forward and forcing Kallus back until the demon had nowhere to go with his back pressed against the wall. "What do you think will happen if I touch you?" Baptiste asked, trailing his fingers along Kallus' jaw. Kallus flinched. When no madness entered Baptiste's gaze, the demon's eyes widened. Baptiste didn't give him time to respond. "Do you think I'll immediately fill with greed to have you? That the need will drive me insane and I'll spend my nights shaking and crying your name?" Baptiste went flush against him, holding his mate's stare. He wanted Kallus to see the truth in his eyes. "I've already done those things. So, touch me, Kallus. All I feel is hatred." Baptiste cupped the demon's face, ensuring he couldn't look away. "You make me sick, but not with want. Unless you mean wanting you to hurt. That, you deserve. No one should look at you or touch you and immediately crave you. All you deserve is pain. Hopefully, you'll find it here." Baptiste backed away and flashed Kallus a smile that felt evil even to himself. "Enjoy your stay."

This time, Baptiste's knees really did give out as he crossed the threshold and closed Kallus from his life. Thankfully, Ethan waited for him instead of Dougal. His arms kept Baptiste from collapsing. The man's hard chest cradled him. He saw nothing. His ears no longer worked. Pain tried caving his lungs.

What Dougal called kindness felt a hell of a lot like cruelty to Baptiste. The ringing in his ears subsided as Ethan leeched the emotions from Baptiste, leaving him weak.

Ethan rubbed his back. "I told Dougal I would keep you safe. He was surprisingly understanding and left me to it."

Baptiste inhaled, pulling Ethan's scent into his lungs. "I'm going away." Ethan's arms tightened around him, as if physically trying to stop Baptiste's plans. Baptiste wasn't finished. "Between Eirik's death and this, I think I've stayed too long. Do you think Evan would be okay running the shop?"

Ethan cleared his throat. Baptiste could practically feel the way he was hurting him. "I'm sure he'd be fine. After all, you're always a simple thought away if he has questions, right?"

"Sure," Baptiste said, trying to sound happier than he felt. After all, fake was his middle name these days. Taking a deep breath, Baptiste braced himself for Ethan's rejection. "How do you feel about disappearing with me?" Ethan didn't answer right away. Baptiste didn't blame him. It was asking a lot. Even Baptiste wasn't sure exactly what he was asking for. He could walk away from the demon locked up in the room behind him and never look back, but

Baptiste would still always be a demon's mate. "It's okay." It was too much to ask of anyone. He pulled away and pasted on a fake smile. "I'll come visit."

Ethan's mouth covered his, stopping Baptiste from saying more. There was nothing gentle about the kiss. It was unlike any they'd shared before. Baptiste tasted blood when Ethan bit into his bottom lip. His heart skipped a beat. It was the most he'd felt since Eirik's death. Baptiste found himself shuffling closer. Ethan pulled away. His face was hard. "I'm not a good person," Ethan said, sounding deadly. "You realize that, right? None of my kind are. We feed off drama, pain, and all the passion you can muster. I'm not good."

Baptiste opened his mouth, prepared to argue. Ethan had been nothing but good to him since turning up on his doorstep three years ago.

With a shake of his head, Ethan cut him off. "No, Baptiste. If I go with us, it's not because we're friends. It's because I want you, even though you're not mine. If I go with you, it's because I plan to have you with zero fucks for the beast on the other side of that door."

The heart skipping turned into an unexpected wave of lust. Eirik had been a Viking—a man of action. He conquered. Baptiste was almost ashamed of how much he liked this side of Ethan. "I understand."

"Do you?" Ethan's voice was every bit as hard as his eyes.

Baptiste swallowed. His throat unexpectedly dry. "Yes."

Ethan gave a sharp nod. "Okay. Let's go tell this king goodbye."

As he moved down the hallway, retracing the path Dougal had taken him earlier, Baptiste fought the urge to glance over his shoulder at Ethan. The man's intensity rolled off him in waves. At the mouth of the kitchen, Baptiste paused. His heart slowed at the vision the king's clan presented. Dougal and Faolan wore matching leather braided bracelets. Lire stood, solid, and twisting the men's bracelets, careful not to touch either man's skin. Dougal and Lire smiled, listening to Faolan tell a ridiculous story about cabbage. They loved each other. As Baptiste looked on, Lire took turns bringing the man's wrists to his lips, placing kisses safely on the leather to keep from exposing the men to his curse. Baptiste rubbed his chest. When he'd seen them together earlier in the day, he'd cast his own problems on them and lashed out. Lire had rightfully lashed back. Baptiste got tired of being wrong.

He moved farther into the room, making his presence known.

Jonathan turned from the freezer where he had some odd salt and ice cream mixture going on. "Hey. Are you okay?"

Baptiste nodded. "Could I have two strands of your hair?"

"Excuse me?" Jonathan looked as surprised by the request as he rightfully should.

"You'll have to pull them out. No one else can pluck the hair of a god."

Jonathan blinked. "I'm sorry."

"It's for a spell," he explained, moving to stand beside the three men trying so hard not to touch one another. "May I see these bracelets?" Baptiste asked, motioning toward the leather Lire had been kissing moments earlier.

Unlike Jonathan, the men didn't hesitate. "Sure," Dougal said, untying his and handing it over. Faolan followed suit.

Ethan flashed him a smile and sat at the kitchen table. He knew what Baptiste was about.

Baptiste put the bracelets together, whispering an incantation over the pieces as he moved to Jonathan's side. "Hair, please?"

Jonathan shrugged and yanked out two strands

of hair. "Your grandmother did this for me," Baptiste explained as he unwound the leather strands before weaving the hair through the bracelets. "Not that it did me any good. Kallus walked away before he even knew about it," Baptiste added absently. "A god's hair cannot be broken."

"I'm not a god," Jonathan said as he watched over Baptiste's shoulder.

"No. You're the grandson of a goddess. That makes you even stronger."

"Why did Kallus leave?" Lire asked as he watched Baptiste braiding the leather pieces.

"I don't know," Baptiste answered, keeping his gaze locked on his task. "Eirik died, and he was gone. He never looked back." Baptiste tied off the final piece. "*Diva quibus componuntur Celeste nemo divellunt.* What Goddess Celeste put together, let no man tear asunder." The bracelets shimmered gold for a second before returning to normal. He moved back to Dougal and Faolan and handed back the bracelets. "As long as you're wearing these, you'll be free to touch Lire without any consequences. May you have a life I never could." He turned away before he could see their reactions. His gaze met Ethan's. The man stood. Their hands met, and they disappeared.

Lire stared at the spot where Baptiste had been only moments earlier. "What just happened?"

Warm fingers brushed his cheek. Faolan was touching him. Dougal touched his other cheek. They looked amazed. Faolan broke first. "Holy fook. It's sorcery."

Lire held still, scared to move. Neither man appeared crazed with lust, and his powers weren't being fed. It was just a normal stroke of skin on skin.

"Seriously, what just happened here?" Faolan sounded shocked.

Jonathan tossed his spoon into the sink, dragging all eyes his way. "You just watched a man give you a life that was stolen from him. Go enjoy it. I have a demon to deal with."

Lire's loyalties split straight down the middle at the order. He fought the urge to take his men away to some place they could revel in this new gift. But, if anything happened to Jonathan, all was lost.

"My king," Lire said, feeling defeated. "I can't—"

Jonathan snapped his fingers and Lire stared at the ceiling of the room he shared with Dougal and Faolan. His mates warmed the mattress on either side of him.

"Shit," Lire cursed, scrambling for the edge of the bed. He slammed against an invisible wall around the mattress. "What the fuck?" He tried again, only to find himself on his back. *Jonathan? What the fuck?*

Stay. Jonathan sounded firm. *I'm right down the hall. If anything happens, you'll be free to help. Until then, enjoy Baptiste's gift. You have no idea what it cost him.*

I can't leave you unprotected.

A breeze skirted across Lire's skin, as if Jonathan caressed him with his mind. *I'm not leaving you a choice.*

Lire glanced over his shoulder. Dougal and Faolan wore matching expressions of concentration where they too tried reasoning with Jonathan. Their faces cleared. They exchanged glances. There was nothing they could do. As much as they might be Jonathan's guards, Jonathan was stronger than all of them. If he meant to handle things on his own, they couldn't stop him.

Faolan lifted his arm and inspected the bracelet he wore. "I never thought..."

Lire knew. Faolan didn't need to finish his thoughts. None of them ever expected they'd be able to touch. It felt too good to be true—like the moment they actually set hands on one another, the blessing would slip through their fingers.

They took turns inspecting one another. Dougal smiled. "You both know I love you, right? Like with everything I have."

"Aye," Faolan said while Lire nodded.

"I can't stay in this bed and leave Jonathan unguarded. I owe him everything."

Faolan nodded. "Aye. I want to lounge about and stroke you both until you scream my name. That's not happening until our king is safe."

They exchanged matching determined smiles before diving for the invisible wall. They'd break through if it killed them.

JONATHAN CHECKED THE HOUSE'S PERIMETER AND made small talk in his head with his husbands. He wanted Kallus to stew. This one wasn't like Lire. Jonathan wasn't as sure in his dealings with him. When they spoke, Jonathan could feel Kallus' dishonesty, but he couldn't decide which of his words were lies. After finding the chalk where he'd stashed it earlier, Jonathan headed down the hall again. Outside the door, he hesitated. Baptiste had chosen to help his clan, but it didn't feel like much of a win. He was certain Lire, Dougal, and Faolan would disagree. Jonathan's shoulders still weighed too much. He'd done nothing to help Baptiste. It didn't matter Jonathan recognized there was no comfort for Baptiste in this life. He'd still hoped. Jonathan unbolted the door and strolled inside. Kallus stared out the window. He didn't turn at Jonathan's arrival.

"There's no greed in this house. I'll starve in a few months."

Jonathan settled in the chair he'd occupied earlier. "I'm not sure about that. My mates won't be home for a few more days. I should think this house will be filled with longing until then."

Kallus turned. His light blue eyes stood out brighter than the rest of the room. "That's an extension of love. There's no such thing as greed in real love. All the feelings you have for your mates are derived from your love for them. There's no grasping in that."

Jonathan smiled. "You sound like a bible verse I read once. I never found much comfort in religion before my turning. Of course, I didn't know there was so much to learn about the afterlife."

Kallus snorted and turned his back on Jonathan

again. "You're so young. You're like an infant to me. If you live long enough, you'll stop believing in everything, even if you can see it, touch it, and taste it."

Compared to everyone he knew, Jonathan was like an infant. He couldn't even grasp how old Kallus was, being the first-born son of Mammon. Mammon was as old as time. Kallus couldn't be much younger than that as well.

"As long as you've been alive, you never loved until Baptiste. Why him?"

"I built Baptiste's voodoo shop for him, did you know?" he asked instead of answering Jonathan's question. "There was no avarice in our relationship either. I had to create something that would draw the miserly people in, looking for spells to bring them riches. I fed off their emotions. I've never been anywhere where it was enough—where I felt full. However, there was this one night, too many years ago to count, I was inside this tavern in Rouen. There was this huge mountain of a man, covered in tattoos and scars. He had these piercing light gray eyes that were almost eerie to look at. Everyone gave him a wide berth. His gaze was honed on this tiny mouse of a man. Well," Kallus waved dismissively, "he wasn't really all that small, but compared to this guy, he looked like he'd be crushed. Little Mouse held a book, trying to read by the world's shittiest candlelight. God, it's amazing we're not all blind from those days. Anyhow," Kallus said, turning, claiming his chair, and focusing on Jonathan, as if getting into his story. "The insatiable hunger rolling from this giant in waves was like doing ten lines of coke. The higher I got, the more I wanted. This ravenous longing twisted my insides like nothing I'd ever experienced. I had to have more. So I became one with my new little pet. I ensured he turned his head and met that giant's stare." Kallus shook his head. His smile bordered on insane. "Dear Goddess, the explosion of emotions as their gazes met... there are no words. I didn't need to control either man. All I had to do was go along for the ride. I stayed high for so long, I didn't recognize I'd hung around inside Baptiste too long. I had feelings and shit. They wouldn't go away. The greed had dried up and turned to love. I had to find nourishment elsewhere, but I couldn't stay away. With no real plan, I found ways to insert myself in their lives. This time, as myself, ensuring they fell for me the way I had them." Kallus stayed silent, staring at nothing for so long Jonathan almost poked him. Then, Kallus blinked. When he spoke, the excitement was gone, replaced with only a dead note. "It was a slap in my father's face, having a son capable of falling in love. Then, we were mated, and his fury was like nothing I'd ever seen. I'd switched teams. Goddess Celeste had blessed me—the fifth prince of Hell's son. It couldn't stand. It wasn't done." Kallus' gaze bounced back to Jonathan's. "He came for us with every pack member he could find. One day, Asmodeus will do the same for your demon. In our world, sons obey their fathers or they die. In my case, my gorgeous Viking died protecting us, and my shy little mouse hates me for it."

Jonathan wanted to rage against the unfairness of their world. He would die if anything happened to one of his mates. "It wasn't hatred I felt from Baptiste when he was here earlier."

Kallus shook his head. A sad smile touched his lips. "Trust me, he loathes me. It's the only thing keeping him alive. If it wasn't for my existence, he'd move on to the next life, but he thinks I want my freedom and his death would give it to me. So his hatred forces him from bed each day. Baptiste lives because his life brings me suffering. That's what real unadulterated hatred is like. It hurts him to feel that way about someone he once loved. That's what you feel from him, but make no mistake, it's pure—untainted by a single drop of love."

Jonathan stood and moved to the window, pulling the chalk from his pocket as he went. "Well, I have bad news for you. Malice isn't enough any longer. Before he left, I saw his intentions. He's going away, tidying up loose ends, and moving on to whatever reincarnation he gets next. Ethan will go with him, of course. He'll help ease the pain of Baptiste's passing. Ethan loves him, you know?" Jonathan said over his shoulder, rubbing salt in Kallus' wounds. "He loves him enough to let him go, so Baptiste can find peace. That's more than you can say, I think."

The loudest, fakest, and most obnoxious laughter Jonathan had ever heard sounded from behind him. Jonathan turned, abandoning his plans of setting Kallus free with the appearance of his evil laughter. He focused on Kallus once more. The demon swiped at his eyes. "That was a good one, new king. Really. For someone all-seeing, you're unnaturally blind. Ethan won't be holding Baptiste's hand while he crosses over. Quite the opposite, I imagine. I suggest you kill me now, because once Ethan is done with Baptiste, he'll come for me."

Confusion mixed with impending doom. "What do you mean?"

Kallus' mouth lifted in one corner. "You honestly don't know who Ethan really is, do you?"

Jonathan could only stare at Kallus in wonder. He had a terrible feeling he'd made a huge misstep. Now, all he could do was wait for the other shoe to drop.

5

Ethan glanced around. The room they stood in was constructed of hand carved wood, made in the day when wood was heated and shaped before it cooled. The cabin was huge and had taken years to build. "Sweden?"

Baptiste's eyebrows damn near hit his hairline. Ethan bit back a chuckle at the sight. "How did you know?"

"Lucky guess." He knew everything but chose to keep that to himself. Baptiste looked tired. It had been a long day for him, seeing Kallus again. There were dark circles beneath Baptiste's eyes. Ethan wanted to kiss them away. Baptiste kept running his hand over his short-cropped blond hair. If it were longer, the strands would be standing on end from the abuse. Things had gotten worse lately. Ethan had hoped the more years that passed, the more Baptiste's pain would ease. The opposite was true. It visibly grew with each passing day. He half expected Baptiste to scratch at his skin until he drew blood. Ethan needed to make it stop. He was the only one who could.

Baptiste turned in a circle. "This was Eirik's. I haven't been here in years. Not since he... I should've sold it before now."

"You're selling it?"

Baptiste flashed him a sad smile but didn't respond. Ethan wanted to growl. Before he could respond, he felt a wave of exhaustion roll from Baptiste. Baptiste rubbed his temples.

"When was the last time you fed?"

Baptiste shook his head and turned away. "I'm just tired. After I get some sleep—"

Ethan shifted, moving through space to appear inches from Baptiste. Baptiste lifted his chin and met Ethan's stare. The man's light green eyes punched Ethan in the chest. The way they always did. Ethan had never possessed a great deal of scruples. When it came to Baptiste, his conscience was nonexistent. He wanted him. Ethan wouldn't stop. There was no line he wouldn't cross.

Without a word, Ethan hauled Baptiste against

him and urged his face to his throat. The sound of Baptiste's heartbeat got louder as it sped. His lips brushed Ethan's neck. Ethan's dick stirred. His eyes fell closed. Baptiste's teeth scraped at Ethan's pulse point. A moan clogged Ethan's throat. His hold tightened on Baptiste. He needed this. Baptiste's fangs pierced his skin. The moan fell from Ethan's lips. His cock jumped, aching for more. Baptiste sucked. Ethan grabbed two handfuls of ass and lifted, leaving Baptiste little choice but to wrap his legs around Ethan's waist. Baptiste was hard for him too. There was no hiding it. Possessiveness roared through Ethan. So many times, he'd been a hairsbreadth away from being inside Baptiste, only to have Baptiste stop him or someone interrupt them. Now, in a cabin in the middle of nowhere, Ethan would have this man who completely owned his every thought. It was well past time he claimed Baptiste. The man needed someone to soothe him.

Ethan didn't make it far. He'd been dying of thirst for too long. Some type of animal fur covered the floor in front of the unlit fireplace. Baptiste ripped his fangs away. Ethan took Baptiste to the floor on top of the rug. He tried to be gentle, but the sound of clothing ripping rent the air. The more skin he bared, the more Ethan wanted. He kissed and licked every new inch. Panting breaths filled the air. Ethan no longer knew whose they were. He didn't take from Baptiste. Ethan needed him to feel everything. The beast inside him roared for Ethan to bite, tear into Baptiste's skin and claim the man properly. Ethan fought the voices.

The instant he freed Baptiste's erection, Ethan swallowed him. He took no mercy. The need to fuck with Baptiste's head, the way Baptiste fucked with him, was killing Ethan. They'd never be even. Ethan had been quietly longing for too long. That didn't mean Ethan couldn't try balancing the playing field. Only when he had Baptiste pulling at his hair and begging did Ethan climb up Baptiste's body and claim his mouth. He fully intended to push his way inside with no lubricant other than his spit. Ethan had to get inside Baptiste before the man changed his mind. He swiped his crown across Baptiste's asshole, panting in his desperation. Baptiste turned his head and gasped for air. Ethan's lips collided with Baptiste's cheek. It was wet. He jerked back. Silent tears slipped from Baptiste's eyes. It was like a sledgehammer to the chest. He couldn't breathe. Baptiste still couldn't feel him. Ethan didn't know how to make Baptiste see the truth.

ETHAN FROZE, STARING DOWN AT HIM, LOOKING EVERY bit as disappointed in Baptiste as he was in himself.

"I'm sorry. Don't stop. I want you."

Rather than pushing forward, Ethan's weight settled between Baptiste's thighs. His eyes filled with understanding. It was worse than dying. Baptiste didn't want to stop, but he also couldn't explain how making love to Ethan meant he was letting go of men he'd loved more than life.

"You don't have to be alone," Ethan said, wiping the moisture away from Baptiste's cheek. "You're not alone. I can set you free."

He was such a mess. Ethan deserved better. "I don't understand why you want me. You could have anyone."

Ethan's gaze softened. "I more than want you. I die a little every passing moment I don't have you."

Baptiste stopped breathing. He'd heard those words before. The memory slammed into him like a bulldozer, wrecking him.

They spent every waking moment together. Each one was torture for Baptiste. Eirik never touched him, but he watched Baptiste with open hunger. His heated stare kept

Baptiste on the edge of all-consuming desire and scared to death to make a move.

While sitting in a field of flowers, Eirik avidly listened as Baptiste read. Mid-sentence, Baptiste broke beneath the strain. His gaze shot to Eirik. "You should not watch me as you do."

Eirik's mouth lifted in one corner. "How do I watch you?"

Heat rushed to Baptiste's cheeks. He shouldn't have said anything. His insides shook with nervousness. He dipped his chin to hide his blush. His words came out stuttered. "Never mind. I just..."

A flower touched Baptiste's cheek, bringing his chin up. Eirik brushed the soft petals along Baptiste's jawline. "Tell me how I watch you," Eirik whispered.

Baptiste couldn't look away from Eirik's beautiful gray eyes. He swallowed. He'd never been more scared in his life. Men didn't look at men the way Eirik looked at him, especially men like Eirik—a warrior. He couldn't deny Eirik's request. "Like you want me," Baptiste whispered, bracing for the worst.

Eirik moved onto his knees. He crawled, closing the distance between them until he had Baptiste on his back, and he straddled Baptiste's hips. "I more than want you. I die a little every passing moment I don't have you."

Baptiste stared harder at Ethan, searching for

anything. "It's not possible."

Ethan shifted and brushed his crown across Baptiste's asshole. "Tell me how you feel," he demanded, sounding stern and ratcheting up Baptiste's lust.

"Confused."

Ethan kissed his jaw while still toying with his ass. "I meant physically, gorgeous. Tell me how you feel."

The way Ethan kept using his crown to massage the spot between Baptiste's balls and asshole had his dick leaking like crazy. His mind was a mess. Baptiste licked his parched lips. "Turned on," he whispered, shyness roaring in like a freight train despite everything else.

"Don't be scared. You're with me. Tell me."

Baptiste closed his eyes and focused. "You're killing me. I want to shove my hand between us and jack off. You have me so close to release. But I'm curious too. I need to know if you can make me come by this alone."

Warm lips touched the shell of his ear. Ethan's cock found its way inside just enough to tease him before disappearing again. "You already know I can."

The air in Baptiste's lungs disappeared. He couldn't think. Nothing penetrated his mind. His body was in control. His balls drew up tight. Ethan's cock stretched his asshole again. This time, going deeper before disappearing.

"Do you want it?"

A gasp escaped Baptiste. "Yes." Pressure beat at his crown, screaming for release.

"Say my name."

Baptiste writhed beneath him. He was so close. His body burned. "Ethan."

Ethan's cock gently pushed at Baptiste's asshole, driving him insane. He was right there. Ecstasy lingered right out of reach. "Say *my* name," Ethan demanded.

It didn't make sense. He didn't know how he knew, but he did. "Eirik."

"Good boy," Eirik said, claiming Baptiste's mouth as he took Baptiste's ass—hard. An orgasm roared through him. He couldn't think. Baptiste could only feel. Waves of pleasure rocked him to his core. His soul knew this man, even though he didn't look the same. He didn't understand. It didn't matter. Eirik was there. Three years. It had been three of the longest fucking years. He'd been empty. So goddamn empty. No one could understand. Tears rolled from his eyes. He couldn't stop them.

"Shhh," Eirik whispered against his lips as he

rocked inside him. "I've got you." He kissed
Baptiste's tears. His mouth moved to Baptiste's jaw
before he buried his face in the crook of Baptiste's
neck. Even after release, Baptiste's lust didn't wane.
He needed more. He needed the three years he'd
lost. With two hands buried in the fur beneath him,
Baptiste held on. Teeth scraped his neck. Baptiste's
cock jerked. No one had drunk from him since the
last time Eirik did. Baptiste shook with need. Fangs
pierced his vein. Eirik sucked. Baptiste came again.
Stars popped behind his closed lids. He felt the ties
of their bond tighten, as if Goddess Celeste tied a
new knot in their marriage, holding them together.
Baptiste didn't know how this was possible. He didn't
care. Fate showed its hand, and Baptiste wanted this
in any fucking form he could have it. Answers would
come soon enough. Right now, he just needed this
and nothing else.

Eirik rocked inside him, taking his pleasure and
stealing every piece of Baptiste. His muscles
hardened. Baptiste held on, needing Eirik's orgasm.
When he came, he roared. The sound held as much
triumph as it did pleasure. Baptiste couldn't look
away. He needed every second. As he looked on,
Eirik's eyes changed color, turning from blue to the
swirling gray they'd been before his death. Baptiste's

throat swelled. He couldn't look away from the eyes he never thought to see again. Baptiste stroked Eirik's face. "How is this possible?"

Instead of answering, Eirik kissed him, silencing his questions. "Sleep," Eirik whispered against his lips. Baptiste's eyes grew heavy. "Dream. Remember." At Eirik's command, the world went dark. The flowers were back.

They spent every waking moment together. Each one was torture for Baptiste. Eirik never touched him, but he watched Baptiste with open hunger. His heated stare kept Baptiste on the edge of all-consuming desire and scared to death to make a move.

While sitting in a field of flowers, Eirik avidly listened as Baptiste read. Mid-sentence, Baptiste broke beneath the strain. His gaze shot to Eirik. "You should not watch me as you do."

Eirik's mouth lifted in one corner. "How do I watch you?"

Heat rushed to Baptiste's cheeks. He shouldn't have said anything. His insides shook with nervousness. He dipped his chin to hide his blush. His words came out stuttered. "Never mind. I just..."

A flower touched Baptiste's cheek, bringing his chin up. Eirik brushed the soft petals along Baptiste's jawline. "Tell me how I watch you," Eirik whispered.

Baptiste couldn't look away from Eirik's beautiful gray eyes. He swallowed. He'd never been more scared in his life. Men didn't look at men the way Eirik looked at him, especially men like Eirik—a warrior. He couldn't deny Eirik's request. "Like you want me," Baptiste whispered, bracing for the worst.

Eirik moved onto his knees. He crawled, closing the distance between them until he had Baptiste on his back, and he straddled Baptiste's hips. "I more than want you. I die a little every passing moment I don't have you."

"I want you too." At Baptiste's confession, Eirik's eyes changed. They'd always been light, but now they swirled, as if thunder clouds lived inside his irises.

Baptiste's breath caught at the sight. He cupped Eirik's face. "What are you, really? You're more than a vampire. I can feel it."

"I'm yours," Eirik said, lowering his head and capturing Baptiste's lips. Their tongues stroked. Baptiste couldn't breathe past his overwhelming happiness and desire. In Eirik's hold, all his dreams were coming true. Eirik spoke against his lips. "I wish for you to be mine too. Will you stop me?"

Baptiste shook his head. "Don't stop."

The scene shimmered and changed. He was in Canada where they'd lived after Rouen.

Eirik's arms encircled his waist, pulling him back

against his broad chest. "What are you doing today, Little Mouse?"

A smile that was out of his control pulled at the corners of Baptiste's mouth. "I'm writing down some of my minor spells for Dante. They won't do much for him without magic in his blood, but some things are based more on ingredients than magic."

With his face pressed to Baptiste's neck, Eirik inhaled. "You have a little of the devil in you today."

Baptiste didn't respond. He felt it too.

Eirik spun Baptiste in his arm, forcing him to meet his stare. "I know you feel him," he said as he backed Baptiste against the counter. "You like having him inside you, methinks. He gives you the freedom to do things you wouldn't normally do. What would you like to do today?"

Instead of speaking and ruining the moment, Baptiste's hands slid to Eirik's waist. As he looked on, Eirik's eyes changed, swirling with clouds again. Baptiste set his sexy man's erection free. "I'll tell you what's inside me, if you tell me what's inside you," Baptiste said as he dropped to his knees. He didn't look away from Eirik's stare as he licked the man's cock. One day, they'd share all their secrets. Maybe it wouldn't be today, but one day.

The scene changed again. This time, everything was dark. He shook. Fear owned him and choked him, leaving him cold and paralyzed. Their home was no longer a haven. It was a prison. Evil had invaded.

Kallus was on the edge of death. Baptiste could feel his mate's life slipping away. Baptiste fought against the ropes keeping him bound to the chair. Magic weaved through the bindings. He didn't understand. How had demons learned to do such a thing? The door burst open. Eirik's large frame filled the doorway. Relief warred with fear at the sight of his powerful Viking. He knew Eirik would keep him safe if he could. This was one time when Baptiste needed to save Eirik. He'd give his life for his mates. These demons would not take everything from him as long as there was breath in his body.

"Baptiste," Eirik cried, crossing the room and dropping to his knees. He fought to untie Baptiste's wrists.

"Go," Baptiste argued. "It's not me he wants."

Eirik ignored him. He managed to free one arm before the smoke swirled to life behind him.

"Go," Baptiste screamed. His throat felt as if it shredded. His life meant nothing without his mates.

Eirik flew to his feet, spinning as the smoke took the shape of a man. His body shielded Baptiste from attack.

"Where is the key?" The benevolence in the disembodied voice filling the room sent chills down Baptiste's spine. He was after Eirik, but it was obvious Mammon hadn't gotten that information from Kallus.

His poor Kallus. Baptiste fought against his restraints. He needed to help his mates.

Eirik laughed, ridiculing Mammon and keeping the demon's attention locked on him. "Not here."

"I've already tortured quite a bit of information from my spawn," Mammon said, sounding pleased as he motioned toward where Kallus sat, chained and unconscious across the room. "Now I have your Druid. I feel confident—between the two—I can find the key without you."

Eirik smirked. "He knows nothing." As Eirik made the claim, he brushed his fingertips across Baptiste's forehead, stealing the secrets and memories they'd shared. He left behind only enough Baptiste still knew they were married. Eirik left their love untouched. Baptiste felt the rest float away. He shook with fear. Mammon was in their home. Kallus looked dead. Baptiste searched for any signs of life. How had they ended up here? He couldn't remember.

Mammon's eyes were fixed upon Baptiste, looking crazed with rage. "No! What have you done?"

Eirik laughed, sounding triumphant. "Stolen everything," he taunted while keeping Baptiste protected with his huge body. "There's nothing here for you. Kill us all. It matters not. You'll never find what you came for here."

"Then you're no longer needed." A giant sword, made of the same smoke as Mammon, appeared in the demon's hands.

A bright light blinded him, stealing his sight, as if Baptiste's mind shielded him from the grisly images of Eirik's death. When vision returned to him, Mammon was gone and Eirik was dead. Celeste stood over him. She stroked his face. "I will bring him back to you. I pray your pain doesn't steal your ability to recognize him when he returns, but I can't let you keep the memory of what you've seen here. You'll never be safe if I do." The ropes binding him disappeared. Baptiste couldn't look away from Eirik's body. Bile rose in his throat. His life was gone. Everything was gone. As he looked on, Celeste bent over Eirik's headless body. A bright light sifted from Eirik into her hand. The light transformed into a golden key she placed in her pocket. Nothing would penetrate Baptiste's pain and shock. He couldn't think straight or move. Celeste moved back to his side and swiped her hand over Baptiste's hair. The horrible visions of watching Eirik die drifted away. Nothing could take away the pain. Baptiste's body unfroze. He dropped to his knees beside Eirik's body. Demons had been here. He could smell them. Kallus was tied and unconscious in the corner. Baptiste could smell his blood. Celeste stood over him, trying to comfort him. He didn't understand what had happened. It seemed as if the more people who touched him, the more confused he became. Nothing made sense.

Celeste touched his shoulder, bringing his gaze her way. "If only I'd been here sooner. I'm so sorry, Baptiste."

"What's happened?" Bewilderment and shock wouldn't let Baptiste think straight.

"Demons attacked," she explained. "Kallus needs help. He's suffered a lot of damage."

Baptiste had never felt more helpless. Eirik was gone and he couldn't touch Kallus to help him. "I don't know what to do."

Celeste removed a necklace she wore and plucked a hair from her head. She whispered something in a language he didn't understand as she wove her hair through the necklace. It shimmered gold. "Don't forget this spell," Celeste said as she worked. "One day, you'll know in your heart when you need to pass this same gift along to others." She quickly draped the necklace over his shoulders. "As long as you are wearing this necklace, you'll be free to touch Kallus without consequences. For now, I'll take him with me. He needs more help than you can give him. When he's healed, he will return to you."

Baptiste nodded. He wanted to scream his denial. He'd already lost one mate, and she planned to take the other. His throat wouldn't work. He held Eirik's lifeless hand, incapable of doing anything else. In his mind, he rushed to Kallus and tended to the mate he could save. In reality, his body wouldn't budge. There was too much pain. It hobbled him. He'd never dreamed anyone could feel such loss and still breathe beneath the weight.

As he looked on, Celeste crossed the room and lifted Kallus as if he weighed nothing. She met his gaze. "Help will be here soon. Don't move." She disappeared, leaving him alone with nothing.

Time passed without his presence. Even when the door flew open, revealing two identical men Baptiste had never seen, he didn't move. If they were there to kill him, he would be glad for their mercy. The men rushed to his side.

One covered Eirik's body with a blanket, stealing him from Baptiste, while the other pulled him to his feet, wrapping his strong arms around Baptiste. He cared not. Nothing mattered. "I am Ethan," the one holding him said. He motioned the other man's way. "This is my brother, Evan. Eirik called out for us. We came as fast as we could."

Something about the man's claim seemed wrong. In his shock, Baptiste couldn't think straight enough to decipher anything. The room spun. Baptiste couldn't cope. Ethan's arms tightened around him as Baptiste lost consciousness.

6

"I feel something. Right here," Lire said, fingering the invisible wall surrounding their bed. It felt like he'd poked his finger through tightly stretched plastic wrap. "I think I have it. The air feels different." They all concentrated on the same spot. The room spun. All the air squeezed from Lire's lungs. Reality shifted. Lire found himself landing with a hard thump on Jonathan's bedroom floor in a tangle of arms and legs. Faolan, Dougal, and Lire scrambled to disentangle themselves and come to their feet. He caught a quick glimpse of Jonathan's outrage.

"Are you fucking kidding me?"

As quickly as it happened, it was over. Lire panted from exertion as he stared at the ceiling of his bedroom with Faolan and Dougal at his side. They were back in their bed.

"Didn't expect Cin and Niall to be home early," Dougal said, pointing out what they were all thinking.

"Aye."

"Yep," Lire said, feeling like an ass.

"Holy shit, though," Faolan said, bringing up the other elephant in the room.

"Yep."

"Aye."

Lire cleared his throat. "Jonathan is..."

"Aye."

"Aye," his men agreed.

They kept their gazes locked on the ceiling. Lire cleared his throat. "I want to try that."

"Aye."

"Yep."

They exchanged glances. Lire's smile grew along with Faolan's and Dougal's. As one, they scrambled to strip. Now that he knew Jonathan would be fine, Lire couldn't get undressed fast enough. The instant he was nude, Lire snagged the backs of Dougal's and Faolan's heads, pulling them in for a kiss. When their tongues entwined, his heart squeezed in his chest. Time stood still as the beauty of the moment washed over him. This would be their first time. He wished he could think of something powerful to say, letting these amazing men know how their love humbled him.

Faolan ended up being the one with the words. "I've lived a verra long time and loving both of you has been my life's best part."

"Same," Lire whispered as Dougal gasped, "Aye."

Dougal's gasp had more to do with Lire's handling his cock than anything else. He loved making Blondie breathless and Ginger moan. Each man made a different sound that melted Lire.

Faolan dropped his mouth to Lire's shoulder and kissed. He spoke against Lire's skin. "You've been inside me. I think it's only fair I get to be inside you." As he made the claim, he urged Lire onto his side. The air caught in Lire's lungs. He wanted everything. Faolan molded against his back, probing at his asshole. Pants left Lire's lips. His gaze wouldn't move from Dougal. Dougal watched everything as if he couldn't get enough of seeing his men together.

Lire couldn't take not having them both. It had been too long since he'd used his body to please Dougal. "I need to be inside you," he growled as Faolan pressed his way past the tight ring of muscles surrounding Lire's asshole.

Dougal wasted no time throwing his leg over Lire's and Faolan's hips, giving Lire access to his body. It felt like it had been forever since they'd spent their nights in a tangle of sweat, hair, and kisses. This was the first time he could make love to Dougal without ruining the man's mind. The moment was humbling and hot. He licked his fingers and stretched Dougal's asshole as he fought to hang on to his sanity with Faolan pumping inside him at the perfect angle. Lire had lived a long time. Being a sex demon meant there was nothing he hadn't done a million times. This was the first time a threesome completely wrecked his heart. He knew, as long as he lived, he'd never forget this first time of making love to his mates with his body or the sound Dougal made as Lire pushed his way inside. They moved slowly, keeping time with one another. Inside, Lire was crazed. He refused to show his madness. His mates deserved to have him make love to them— slowly savoring each second.

With his forehead pressed to Dougal's, they strained toward release. Faolan's emotions were drowning Lire. He was every bit as overwhelmed as Lire. They'd been given so much. Lire had never had more to lose. His body was ablaze with need. He stroked Dougal's cock, completely convinced that if the man came, the pleasure would be his. Dougal's breathing increased. His muscles tightened. They were right there, together. Lire's balls drew up tight.

Faolan's fingers dug into Lire's skin. "Goddamn, gorgeous. You fook with my head. You're so hot on my dick."

Lire's stomach muscles clenched. Faolan's words had him on edge. Then, Dougal's cum hit him in the chest as the man's orgasm slammed into Lire's mind. Being connected in body and mind was explosive. A cry tore from Lire's lips. Faolan slammed home, hitting at the perfect angle, stealing Lire's orgasm. Faolan cried out. His fangs brushed Lire's neck, as if he barely fought the urge to tear into Lire's skin, despite his acidic blood. Lire melted, turning to smoke and becoming one with Faolan, even though he didn't have to anymore. He needed Faolan fangs in Dougal's neck, so he could savor the blood exchange. His mates could never drink directly from him or vice versa, but it didn't matter. He could have this and so much more. Dougal's blood filled Faolan's mouth. The coppery tang danced on Lire's taste buds. Love filled him until he thought he'd explode. With his needs met, Lire separated from Faolan and fell into a tangle of sweaty arms and legs. He snuggled closer, uncaring of the mess they'd made. It was real, raw, and all them. He owned the world.

Guilt wasn't a word that lived in his vocabulary, but as Lire snuggled with Dougal and Faolan, he felt the first kernel. He'd pushed his way inside Baptiste's mind, seeing more than he intended. What he'd done was cruel, especially in light of Baptiste's kindness. The man had given Lire this moment, and countless more to come. Jonathan was right. Lire didn't fully comprehend what it had cost the man. He hoped he never learned. Losing his mates wasn't a fate he could fathom. He couldn't imagine the man's hopelessness. All he knew was—somehow—he'd find a way to repay Baptiste one day.

EIRIK SPENT A MINUTE ENJOYING WATCHING BAPTISTE sleep after he carried him to bed. It had been so damn long. He wished he could stay there forever, but he had business to attend to. "Don't worry, my little mouse. Everything will be right again." He slipped from the bed and lit a fire in the fireplace before clothes appeared on his body.

A howl sounded in the distance. Eirik headed

out. The minute he stepped outside, a giant silver wolf appeared. In an instant, he transformed into a large, nude male with silver hair. No lines marred his face, making his hair color look unnatural. Bleidd Gunnolf was every bit as old as Eirik. They'd grown up together back when the world was new. He trusted Bleidd's pack above all others to keep his mate safe.

"I won't be long."

Bleidd nodded. "Don't worry about Baptiste. We'll watch over him."

"You have all my faith. Still, this shouldn't take long." With that promise hanging in the air, Eirik shifted through space, appearing in Jonathan's living room. He wouldn't wait for an invite. Jonathan sat curled in a huge leather chair in the laps of his mates. A blanket covered them. His blond mate slept while his dark mate toyed with Jonathan's hair. Jonathan glanced up from the book he was reading. He looked more human today than Eirik had ever seen him before. His wings were gone, and his eyes were green rather than the usual gold.

As Eirik's form solidified, a loud siren rent the air. Jonathan snapped his fingers, and the alarm fell silent. Cin came awake with a start, but Jonathan soothed him by rubbing his chest. Niall never paused in toying with Jonathan's hair.

Dougal, Faolan, and Lire appeared, nude but armed to the teeth. Jonathan sighed when he saw them. "Jesus, it's like no one listens to me."

Despite having closed his eyes again, Cin grumbled, "Everything is fine. Get back to bed."

The men's shoulders fell—like they'd been robbed of a good battle. The ginger of the bunch spoke up. "I see how it is. When we're clothed, we get snapped back to bed. Naked, we have to make the walk of shame."

Jonathan flashed the men an adorable smile. "Maybe I enjoy watching your sexy nude asses leave."

At his claim, all three men slowed in their departure and a visible hip sway entered their walk. Jonathan chuckled as the three disappeared. He waited until they were gone before focusing on Eirik once more. "I keep telling them to stay in bed, but they keep disobeying me today."

Eirik bit back a smile. "Well, they are your guards."

"I don't need protection today," Jonathan said. His unconcerned air might've chafed if he'd meant the man harm. It was obvious Jonathan didn't fear him.

"You have something that belongs to me."

Jonathan nodded and reopened the book he'd dropped to soothe Cin. "You know the way."

Eirik dipped his chin and headed down the hall. Jonathan was a puzzle he couldn't decipher. Not only was it obvious Jonathan knew who he really was, he also seemed to have known Eirik would come for Kallus. Outside the room where Kallus was held, Eirik didn't hesitate. He threw open the door with enough force it bounced from the wall. Kallus sat slumped in a chair with his arms crossed over his chest. At Eirik's arrival, he straightened. His hungry gaze ate up the sight of Eirik as if he saw past the Ethan image to the god housed beneath.

Without wasting time, Eirik clapped. The thunderous sound it created destroyed the wards inside the room, freeing Kallus. "Let's go." He didn't wait to see if his mate obeyed. Eirik knew he would. Retracing his steps, he found Jonathan where he'd left him.

Jonathan didn't look up from his book. "Once you've gotten everything settled, I expect a solid explanation." He finally glanced up from his book. His face and voice hardened, becoming the leader

Celeste had chosen him to be. "Or don't return here. I've had my throat slit, my heart almost ripped out, and my mate kidnapped. We spent months sweeping up the bodies. All because of your issues. So you will explain or you won't come back. Understood? We can help, or you can stay away."

Eirik dipped his chin. It was a fair trade, considering all Jonathan had sacrificed. For now, he needed to return to Baptiste. Thankfully, Baptiste slept on. Eirik's earlier order to remember held him in its grip. After peeking at his dreams, ensuring they were of happy times, Eirik moved to the settee, where he could keep an eye on him. Kallus followed him, holding his silence. Eirik couldn't bring himself to look the man's way. The only safe place to look was at Baptiste's sleeping form. Even as Kallus settled in beside him, Eirik couldn't turn his head and meet his mate's gaze.

"How long do you plan on not talking to me?"

Eirik watched Baptiste's chest rise and fall with each breath while he thought about the question. It wasn't that he wasn't on speaking terms with Kallus as much as he feared his voice. For three years, he'd been bound by Mammon's presence, sticking close to Baptiste, keeping him safe but incapable of touching his mate as himself. He'd been forced to try to woo the man under the worst of circumstances, keeping his powers hidden so Mammon wouldn't sense him. Then Jonathan had banished Mammon back to Hell, freeing Eirik. By then, he'd told too many lies. He'd held his silence while watching Baptiste suffer. His actions, while meant for Baptiste's protection, were unforgivable. Chances were good Baptiste would wake—memories intact and hating Eirik. Being enraged with Kallus gave him an outlet for his fear. While Eirik had done the best he could with the choices available to him, Kallus had simply walked away. Were they equally guilty? Yes, but Eirik's rage still knew no bounds.

"He'll have questions when he wakes," Eirik said rather than answering.

"Do you have answers?"

Eirik took a breath and chose not to respond.

"Like now, with me," Kallus pushed. "Can you explain why I spent days being tortured for you, until Baptiste found me, yet you never once came to me after Celeste created a new form for you? Can you answer that one? Was I the lesser mate to you?"

Eirik's eyes fell closed. He'd fallen in love, given himself a weak point, and created a target for Mammon. He didn't regret falling in love with Baptiste and Kallus. Not only would he do it again in a minute, he fully intended to win back his mates. An overheated weight landed on him. His eyes flew open. Kallus straddled his hips and held his face between his hands, leaving him no choice but to look at him. The man's beauty hit Eirik in the chest.

"Say it, Eirik. Tell me I never meant that much. Say you hate me for bringing evil into your life."

Pain ripped through him. "I cannot."

Kallus' expression screamed how much Eirik was hurting him. "Then tell me why I mean so little."

Eirik gripped the back of Kallus' neck and hauled him forward, capturing his mate's lips for the first time in over three years. Nothing had changed. He still loved these men with all that he was. He tore his mouth away but kept his forehead pressed to Kallus' and a tight grip on the man's neck. "I was ashamed," he admitted with his eyes squeezed shut. "Everything is because of me. If I'd stayed away from the two of you, none of this would've happened. All of this is on me. How could I look at you after the pain I caused?"

"I feel the same," Kallus said, taking him by surprise. "I'm a demon. If anyone should've known better, it's me. I should've known loving you and Baptiste was power my father wouldn't be able to resist. Now I've lost you, and Baptiste hates me more than anything I've ever witnessed."

The backs of Eirik's eyes stung. "You haven't lost me, and Baptiste doesn't hate you."

Kallus' eyes fell closed for a second. When they reopened, the other man's pain was almost a physical thing. "He touched me and felt nothing. I've never seen that. All I felt was his anger."

Despite the situation, a smile touched Eirik's lips. "That was an evil move on his part. Celeste gave him the power to touch you without consequences," Eirik explained when Kallus still looked broken. "Did she not tell you?"

Kallus blinked several times, as if trying to come to terms with what he was hearing. "I never saw her. After you... When I woke up, there was an angel tending to me. I was, understandably, confused to find myself in the Heavens. I asked several questions, but no one spoke to me or met my gaze. Once I was fully healed, I was set free."

Eirik ran his fingers through Kallus' hair. "He's angry with you, but you'll convince him to forgive you. You know Little Mouse never stays mad for long." His gaze dropped to Kallus' mouth. He couldn't stop himself from brushing his thumb along the man's bottom lip. "If I didn't already know hell existed, these past three years have shown me suffering only the damned endure. But I knew it could be worse and knowing I was the reason Mammon harmed you again was too much for me. I wonder if you'll ever forgive me, or if I'll ever forgive myself?"

Kallus visibly swallowed. "Kiss me again, and we'll see."

Moving slow, Eirik drew Kallus closer. His lips tingled with anticipation. He was so close to having his mates again. He could practically taste the triumph.

A loud gasp sounded from the bed. At the sound, they scrambled from the couch. Baptiste sat straight up—like a shock raced through his body. He gasped for air while blinking rapidly as if trying to bring the room in to focus. Before Eirik could reach his side, Baptiste was gone.

Eirik and Kallus stopped in their tracks, staring the empty spot where Baptiste had been. Kallus turned in a circle as if physically and mentally searching for Baptiste. "He's gone to Jonathan."

Eirik nodded. "Give him a minute. I removed the block Celeste and I created in his mind. Let him think straight. If he doesn't come back, we'll go after him."

Their gazes met. A silent conversation passed between them. Despite Eirik's earlier bravado, they knew the truth. Baptiste might not ever forgive them.

NIALL'S FINGERS BRUSHED THROUGH JONATHAN'S HAIR. Jonathan couldn't tear his gaze away from his mate's amazing eyes. He loved his dark warrior. Times like these, when they could enjoy one another uninterrupted, felt few and far between. Cin's hand slid up Jonathan's inner thigh, snaking up the inside of his workout shorts. Jonathan intentionally hadn't worn underwear underneath. Not only did underwear not give as much if he spontaneously went full Nephilim, he loved watching the moment Cin realized he was free to toy with Jonathan's body. It seemed crazy they were incapable of getting enough of one another. He understood this was how mating worked. It was a bond that grew stronger with every passing day. Still, it seemed he should be sick of being constantly touched. Instead, he craved more.

The alarm sounded, startling Jonathan's heart into his throat. Baptiste appeared feet away, wearing nothing more than a blanket. Their gazes met, and

Baptiste collapsed—unconscious. Cin scrambled to his feet. Lire, Dougal, and Faolan skidded into the room, only half as armed as last time, as if expecting to get sent away again. Instead, Jonathan waved them closer.

"It's Baptiste." He skimmed the man's mind. "Whoa. Eirik removed the barrier from his mind. He's a fucked-up mess in there. Let's find a room for him."

Niall scooped the man from the floor and carried him down the hall. They followed, equally ready to circle like a group of meddling hens.

"I thought Eirik was dead," Dougal said behind him, reminding Jonathan he hadn't shared what he'd learned with anyone.

"You can't kill Eirik. He is the first-born son of Heimdall," Baptiste said, proving—while still mostly out of it—he was awake. "As a full-blooded Norse god, he was given the task of being the guardian of Heaven's door. He is the key between the worlds. Like energy, he can't be destroyed, only transformed."

Niall settled Baptiste on a guest bed. Baptiste leaned his back against the headboard and tried catching his breath. Jonathan kept a close eye on his every heartbeat. He didn't want the man falling out again. Everyone stared at the man, hanging on his every word.

Dougal didn't let up. "I don't understand. What about Evan? I thought they were twins."

Baptiste shook his head. "When Eirik died, Celeste retrieved his soul and shaped him into the first guard she encountered, Evan. She made him swear not to reveal anything to me. They told me they were Prampires, explaining how they had no need for blood."

"Prampires died out centuries ago," Faolan said, pointing out what they were all thinking.

"Actually, that's not true. They're just very good at staying hidden. But it was a good cover story, so I wouldn't realize Evan is a werewolf, and explaining how Ethan could leech away my pain from losing my mates."

"Obviously, he wasn't really doing that," Jonathan pointed out.

Baptiste rubbed his chest. "Yeah. I just hurt less when Eirik held me, even with him blocking himself from me."

Lire shook his head. "I'm a demon, and the depth of betrayal here..."

"Aye," Faolan said, sounding every bit as horrified.

"I know." Baptiste's voice sounded heavy with pain. He scrubbed at his arm and massaged his hands. Jonathan couldn't believe the man's mates would do this—leave him in this state.

Eirik and Kallus appeared on either side of Baptiste, stealing Jonathan's chance to say as much. "I'm—once again—retrieving what's mine," Eirik said, obviously intent on disappearing with Baptiste again. The alarm was going nuts, making everyone deaf and Jonathan's nerves bad. Before Eirik could get away, Jonathan shot forward and grabbed hold of Eirik and Kallus, keeping them from going anywhere.

"That's enough of that. It's about time you stayed still. I'm not putting up with this popping in and out all night."

"No offense, but this is none of your business," Eirik said, enraging Lire.

"Look here, I don't give a damn what kind of god you are. You're not allowed to insult our king." Everyone tried yelling over everyone else, making Jonathan's head pound.

"Enough," Niall roared, slamming his fist down on the footboard of the bed and cracking the wood. Everyone fell silent. He wasn't finished. "I've been gone two weeks," he said, holding up two fingers.

"All I want is to curl up with my men and enjoy some peace. Is that too much to ask? This is our home," Niall said, fixing Kallus, Baptiste, and Eirik with his dark gaze. "Do you get that? Just because you're powerful enough to go anywhere you like, doesn't mean you should without asking."

"To be fair, I'm sort of getting dragged along here," Kallus said, sounding petulant.

Baptiste growled. "By all means, feel free to run back to whatever and whoever you were doing before Lire scooped you up."

"I picked him up outside your house, pacing and practicing his speech to win you back."

"What?" Baptiste and Jonathan said simultaneously.

Lire nodded. "He was being quite loud. I don't know how you couldn't hear him."

Jonathan massaged the spot between his eyes. "We brought him in for abandoning his mate, and you picked him up when he was about to go back?"

Lire shrugged. "You didn't tell me why you wanted him."

"What the fook has been going on while I was in Scotland?" Niall asked, bringing all eyes his way.

Jonathan twisted his fingers. "I was unsupervised too long."

Niall stared at him expressionless.

Jonathan took a deep breath. He was so getting spanked later, and he couldn't wait.

"I'm going to bed."

Jonathan nodded. "Okay, I—"

"I expect you there in the next five minutes," Niall said, cutting him off. He switched his gaze Lire's way. "Take your men back to bed like Jonathan's been telling you all goddamn day." Lire nodded, and the three disappeared. Niall pinned the three men in the bed beneath his dark stare. "You can stay here or go home. I don't care. But whatever you decide, the next time you visit, you'll use the damn door like normal fooking people. We've never disrespected your home, and I expect the same. Jonathan is not your personal plaything. He's *mine*. His time is *mine*. Everything under this roof is *mine*. I did not waltz into town and throw my power around, but so help me, I will make you sorry if you do not give my husband peace."

Jonathan spent a lot of time turned on, but Niall's anger had him hotter than he could remember being in a long time. He could barely breathe beneath the onslaught of desire.

"You lucky bastard," Kallus muttered beside him, making Jonathan smile.

He patted Kallus' chest. "Goodnight." Without looking back, Jonathan followed Niall from the room —like an invisible chain tethered him. They knew what was going on and understood now what they were up against. The three men could work out the rest on their own. Jonathan had a punishment to endure. He fully intended to get right on that and beg for forgiveness, or more. Whatever.

———

HE'D LEFT FOR A REASON. NOW HERE EIRIK AND Kallus were, invading his space and making it impossible for him to think. Under his breath, Baptiste chanted a spell, making it impossible for Eirik to take him without his permission. The men disappeared before immediately reappearing when they realized Baptiste wasn't with them.

Eirik's face was thunderous with outrage. "I'm trying to make things right."

"I left for a reason." Baptiste words came out in a growl. He couldn't hide his aggravation if he tried. There was no holding back his anger. "Three years. Three fucking years," he said, ready to punch someone. Baptiste switched his gaze between the men, ensuring they recognized his fury was meant for them both. "Someone start talking. Explain why you would do this to me."

"I didn't want to give Mammon any reason to keep coming after you," Kallus said, speaking up first.

"He did anyway," Baptiste said, exploding despite his continued internal lectures to calm down. "And just as I did before, I walked away without a scratch. Do you have no faith in me, or was I just that easy to throw away once Eirik was gone?" Baptiste didn't give him time to answer before turning his rage Eirik's way. "And you, I don't even know where to start. You were right there, watching me suffer. Why?"

"I'm the reason Kallus was tortured and the two of you were almost killed. The wolves were after Mammon on my order. I kept thinking the danger would pass any day and I wouldn't have to fear putting you in danger any longer. It never crossed my mind it would take three years to be free of Mammon."

"None of this is explaining anything," Baptiste roared, surprising even himself by the explosiveness of his anger. "I'm perfectly capable of handling myself. There's twelve hundred years of my people's magic living inside me, topped with the power of vampires. I'm not afraid. Every day, I relished the thought of Mammon returning, because I knew I could finish the fight. Why don't you believe in me as I've always believed in both of you?"

Eirik stroked his face. "Little Mouse, you shouldn't have to fight."

It was the wrong move and the wrong words. Baptiste scrambled from the bed. He watched the men's gazes turn hungry as they eyed his nude body. Baptiste hated that their expressions made his heart skip a beat. Anger was all he had right now. They'd left him. Maybe it had been in different ways, but they'd abandoned him to his pain and emptiness. With every thought, his fury grew until it couldn't be contained.

"Why can't you admit you think I'm weak?" Baptiste slammed his hand down, further cracking the wooden footboard. "Did you switch your guard duty between Kallus and me, or did you leave him unguarded?"

Neither man spoke, but they visibly fought not to look at each other. He didn't need them to answer. Baptiste knew there was no way Eirik had spent every day with him and guarded Kallus.

Even to Baptiste's ears, he sounded tired when he spoke again. "I would've gladly died for either of you, but I can live without you. These past three years have definitely taught me that. It's beyond obvious neither of you needs me, so you can just keep it that way."

Baptiste moved through space, landing in his living room. He chanted under his breath, locking his house down with ancient Druid spells. His feet moved quickly from room to room. Baptiste didn't think it likely they'd give him much of a head start. By the time he finished, there was no chance anyone other than himself could enter the home. He couldn't trust anyone any longer. Baptiste was finally alone. The pain was swift, nearly doubling him over. There was no Ethan to leech it away. He should've known something wasn't right about the twins. Evan's presence never soothed Baptiste.

Baptiste rubbed his arms. His skin felt chilled—like he'd never be warm again. The lack of clothes didn't help. With no real plan, Baptiste headed for the bathroom. After flipping the stopper closed, he turned the water in the Jacuzzi tub to as hot as it would go. Steam rose with the water. He should've been scalded as he stepped in, but Baptiste felt nothing beyond his internal pain. Kallus and Eirik had each other. He had no one. It was hard to say who angered him most. Baptiste leaned back, letting the water engulf him. Kallus had abandoned him, but at least he'd openly walked away. Eirik had hidden, equally yet just as willfully stealing his love and affection. He'd broken Baptiste down, making him believe he was moving on with another man. There were so many lies. So much deception. Baptiste didn't know how to move past this. What if he never could? If there was a place lower than having no hope, Baptiste was there.

7

A chiming interrupted Cin's story about the Scottish games he'd won. Jonathan glanced around, trying to figure out where the sound came from before giving up and going back to enjoying the way Cin's mouth moved when he spoke.

"How shocked were they when you hit the thing dead center?"

Cin ran his fingers through Jonathan's hair, smiling. "What makes you think I did?"

Jonathan shrugged. He loved these moments, curled up in their favorite chair, stroking and soaking up one another. They'd lost Niall five minutes earlier to his latest sword creation. Jonathan didn't mind. He just wanted to hear every detail of the minutes he'd missed. "You always win."

"Could you love a loser?"

Jonathan cuddled closer, needing more. "If you lost, yes."

The chiming sounded again. This time, Jonathan ignored it. Cin's hands roamed his body. That was all Jonathan cared about. He stroked one of Jonathan's feathers. "Did you know, at least three people asked me questions about your wings. It seems they are perversely fascinated by them." He stroked Jonathan's wing as he made the claim, causing Jonathan's eyes to fall closed. He couldn't describe the sensation of having his wings stroked. It was almost orgasmic.

Dougal strolled by, heading for the front door. "Does nay anyone else hear the doorbell?"

Jonathan's gaze shot to the door. "We have a doorbell?"

Dougal opened the door, and Evan stood on the other side. Jonathan rolled from Cin's lap onto his feet.

"Evan?" Even Jonathan heard the surprise in his voice. "What brings you by?" Jonathan asked as he headed for the door, setting Dougal free.

Evan's smile screamed discomfort. "I was out last night, and when I came home this morning, the house was warded against me."

"Damn," Jonathan muttered under his breath. He took a step back and waved Evan inside. "You'd better come in."

Evan crossed the threshold. "I can't reach anyone and have no idea what's happened."

"I'll be back," Jonathan told Cin as he passed.

Cin kicked back as if prepared to wait.

Jonathan headed down the hall with Evan in tow. "I'm thinking you might want to stay here for a while. Baptiste, Kallus, and Eirik are trying to work things out. It doesn't sound like it's going well." He opened the first bedroom door he knew to be empty. "You can have this room, if you'd like."

Evan glanced inside the empty bedroom before focusing his dark blue gaze on Jonathan. "You know about Kallus and Eirik?"

Jonathan nodded. "And you. Did you know, you're the first werewolf I've ever met. I have so many questions."

Evan chewed on his bottom lip. His gaze swung back to the empty room. "Maybe I should stay with Dante? I don't want to put you out, and all my things are locked up inside Baptiste's."

Jonathan snapped his fingers and Evan's things appeared inside the room. "Stay. We have plenty of room. Just be warned, the guys tend to forget their clothes and you might walk in on anything around here. But, for the most part, everyone pretty much does their own thing." Evan still looked unsure. Jonathan didn't hold back. "Things with Baptiste are pretty ugly right now. Even if they work things out, they probably need some time alone. I promise you're not imposing."

Evan shifted uncomfortably from foot to foot. "Well, my stuff is all here now."

"It is," Jonathan agreed.

"Werewolves roam a lot," Evan warned.

Jonathan nodded. "Good. You can help with patrols."

Evan brightened, as if the idea of helping made him feel like less of an intruder. "I could do that."

Jonathan didn't let up. "In fact, you'd be doing us a huge favor by helping out. We've been overwhelmed lately. Not having enough time off has shortened some tempers. Plus, we've had a lot of people just popping in and setting off the alarms. That kind of thing."

"That's rude," Evan said, making Jonathan's smile grow and strengthening his belief this was the right thing.

"So you'll stay and help?"

Evan eyed his new room and nodded. "I'll stay."

"Good," Jonathan said, determined to get back to Cin. "Feel free to show yourself around. It's your home now, after all." He made it halfway down the hall before Evan called out, stopping him.

"Thank you." Jonathan turned. Evan's sincerity was in his eyes. "Werewolves fall under the rule of the Norse gods, specifically Eirik. I recognize you don't have to help me. So, thank you."

Jonathan dipped his chin, acknowledging his gratitude. "This clan is always accepting good people. You won't let us down." Without waiting for Evan's response, Jonathan headed back to where he'd left Cin. His wings felt neglected. Cin knew how to fix that.

EIRIK STARED AT BAPTISTE'S FRONT DOOR WITH A DEEP line marring his forehead. Baptiste would've laughed if he wasn't so goddamn angry. It couldn't have been more obvious Eirik couldn't find a way around Baptiste's magic. Baptiste stayed hidden behind its wall, watching every move his mate made.

Kallus appeared at Eirik's side. "The store is closed and there's already a 'For Sale' sign in the window."

After scrubbing his hands through his hair, Eirik stared up at the sky, as if seeking guidance. Baptiste rubbed his chest and arms, fighting off the withdrawals. "He could be anywhere by now," Eirik said, dropping his chin and going back to staring at the door. "Or he could be right here, watching every move we make. There's no way to know."

"But I'm so goddamn weak," Baptiste said to himself, sounding childish even to his ears and still not caring. "You'd better figure something out quick. Otherwise, I might die with no real men to protect me. *Pssh*. Such bullshit."

Kallus chewed on his bottom lip as he eyed the door. Neither man realized he stood only feet away. Kallus smiled. Pride shone in his voice when he spoke. "He really is amazing."

"Yep," Baptiste said, walking past them without being seen. "Too bad you didn't realize that sooner." The daylight would keep a normal vampire from dissipating. Baptiste had magic on his side. He didn't use it often any longer. There was never much of a need, but he was still every bit as powerful. He turned, eyeing his mates one last time. His throat swelled. The loss never got easier, but Baptiste had lost them a long time ago. "May Odin grant you knowledge, may Thor grant you strength, may Loki grant you laughter, and may all the Gods remind you every day that I loved you even when you didn't feel the same." Eirik turned at the prayer as if he heard Baptiste's wishes hurdling toward the heavens. Baptiste's eyes blurred at the final sight of light, swirling gray irises. He whispered the words that would take him to his next destination. Even though he had nothing but time, Baptiste was ready to be away from here.

Baptiste appeared on Jonathan's doorstep. For a moment, he blinked at the black wooden surface, trying to call his emotions under control before ringing the doorbell. He'd already looked like a huge fool in front of everyone. Today was a new day. As he pushed the button, a loud musical chime drifted through the air. The door opened, and Lire stood on the other side. His long, curly dark hair fell over one shoulder and his whiskey-colored eyes flashed with surprise at the sight of Baptiste. Of course, Baptiste imagined he probably looked every bit as big of a mess as he felt.

"Hey."

Baptiste managed a small smile. "Hey. Is Jonathan around?"

Lire nodded. "Come in."

Before he could step back, Baptiste waved off the

offer. "No, thanks. I'll wait out here. This won't take long, and I need to be on my way."

The demon started away before pausing and turning back. "I haven't had a chance to thank you for what you did for my mates and me." He looked as uncomfortable as Baptiste felt. Lire cleared his throat. "I also owe you an apology."

"Please, don't," Baptiste said, stopping him. "Just promise me you'll never walk away from your mates, and we're good."

Lire met his stare. "I would rather die than walk away." He meant it.

Baptiste dipped his chin, acknowledging his promise. He was scared to open his mouth. His shit had been barely held together for three years. Today, his strength was at its lowest point. When Lire started away again, Baptiste broke. "They're lucky," he called to Lire's back. Lire glanced over his shoulder and Baptiste couldn't help expounding. "Your mates, they're lucky to have you. I wish you the best." Lire walked away, saving Baptiste from himself. As it was, he was already feeling more uncomfortable than usual, and that was saying a lot. His anger had smothered some of his usual awkwardness, but it was roaring back with a vengeance.

Jonathan appeared in the doorway before Baptiste convinced himself to leave. "Hi," Jonathan said, stepping onto the porch. "How are you doing today? Are things any better?"

For a moment, Baptiste wondered if his throat would work. Finally, he managed to kick his voice into gear. "I came to apologize for dragging you into my problems and ask you to pass my apologies along to Niall. Hopefully, he'll forgive my intrusion last night. I panicked and didn't know where else to go. As you can see, I learned how to use the doorbell." Baptiste managed a small fake smile.

Jonathan didn't look as if he bought it. "Niall is fine. Don't worry over that. If it would make you feel better, you can come in and tell him yourself."

Baptiste shook his head. "I have to go." Baptiste twisted his fingers, feeling inadequate. His gaze skirted past Jonathan as he searched for the right words. Faolan passed by the door. He walked the same as a man on a tightrope. There was a spoon balanced on his nose. For a second, Baptiste lost his train of thought.

At his awkward pause, Jonathan glanced over his shoulder, following Baptiste's line of sight. "Oh, yeah. Cin, sic him." At Jonathan's command, Cin appeared from nowhere, taking Faolan to the floor and sending the spoon flying. The silver piece arced through the air. Baptiste watched it fly past the open door. Jonathan flashed him a sweet smile as if nothing happened. "Are you sure you don't want to come in? I've bet Faolan fifty bucks he can't balance a spoon on his nose for a full ten minutes. So far, I'm winning."

Baptiste cleared his throat. "Um, no. Like I said, I need to go, but I wanted to stop by first and say my goodbyes."

Jonathan's expression turned sad. "Are you not coming back?"

A sad smile tugged at his lips. "I've put the shop up for sale. The house will follow shortly after."

"So, you're not coming back," Jonathan said, saving Baptiste from having to confirm it. He couldn't say the words. New Orleans was his home, but nothing felt right anymore.

"It was very nice meeting you, Jonathan. From what I've seen, you'll be an amazing king." Before Baptiste could walk away, he found himself engulfed in a hug. The relief washing over him as Jonathan's power hit almost took his knees out from underneath him. Baptiste hugged him back before quickly pulling away. He couldn't handle the kindness right now.

"Come visit us," Jonathan said, sounding firm.

Baptiste dipped his chin, even though he didn't mean it, and walked away. He didn't mask his energy for several steps. If Eirik came searching for him, Baptiste wanted the last wisps of his trail to lead away from Jonathan. Hopefully, the king and his clan would be left in peace. At the edge of the woods, Baptiste started his chant, intent on reaching his next destination. Before he could get away, a solid weight hit him in the center of his back, taking him to the ground. Baptiste rolled, ready to defend himself. A large black wolf pounced, pinning him to the ground. In a flash, the wolf transformed, becoming a very nude and pissed-off-looking Evan.

"Where are you going, boss?"

"Um." Baptiste's mind wouldn't work quickly enough.

"Because it kind of looks like you're running away without me," Evan added.

"I—"

"First, you lock me out of the house."

Fuck. He'd forgotten about Evan in his hurt and anger. "Sorry, I—"

"Then you show up here like you're ready to bolt," Evan added, cutting Baptiste off again. "Surely you don't think I've given up three years of my life to watch you run away without me, right?"

Baptiste tried gently pushing Evan away. The man didn't budge. "Well, um, no offense, but I'm not looking for a babysitter."

A deep line appeared between Evan's eyes. "I'm no one's fucking babysitter." He sat back on his heels, forcing Baptiste to try to look anywhere but directly at the man's junk. "Like you said, no offense, but I had a life before I was forced to come here and live this bullshit lie, working at your shop and locked up in the city."

It took everything Baptiste had, but he managed to focus on Evan's eyes. They were Ethan's, but then again, they weren't. Everything about this was so fucking hard. "If you go with me, you'll be separated from everyone. I don't plan to come back, and I'll be damned if you'll go with me if you plan to keep tabs on me for Eirik."

Evan shrugged. "Do you really want to be all alone?"

"I don't know," Baptiste answered honestly. He felt too raw to know himself any longer.

"Well, I don't," Evan said, sounding sad. "You're all I have, and you're dropping me like a stray dog."

Guilt ate at his skin. "Fuck. Come on," Baptiste

said, pushing to his feet. He couldn't leave Evan behind after that. If all else failed, he could always send the man back. For now, maybe they both needed a friend.

———

EIRIK RANG THE DOORBELL, LISTENING AS THE CHIMES filled the air. Stamping feet could be heard through the door, along with cursing. "Goddamn, this is a house of royalty. Can't we get a damn butler? What do you want?" Lire snapped as he threw open the door.

"May we speak to Jonathan?"

"He's too busy to speak with betrayers today. Try back tomorrow."

Eirik spoke through clenched teeth. "It's important or I wouldn't bother him."

"Nope, can't do it," Lire said as he tried shutting the door.

Kallus slapped his hand against the wood, stopping him. "We're looking for Baptiste. We've been tracking his energy. This is the last place he popped up."

"No shit," Lire said, intentionally being unhelpful. "You were with him."

"Not last night," Eirik growled, losing his patience. "This morning."

Lire glanced between them. His lip curled with disgust. "You're killing me with this bullshit," Lire said, practically sneering each word. "You both had no problem leaving him alone before. Now you act as if he won't survive a day without you. It serves you right to suffer some time without him. After all, he's spent three years without you."

"For the last time," Eirik growled. "I was trying to protect him, and he wasn't without me."

The ugliest snort Eirik had ever heard escaped the lust demon. "Is this the condescending shit you fed him? If so, it's no wonder he left."

Eirik swallowed his anger. Losing his temper would get him nowhere. "I'm trying to make it right," he said, enunciating each word. "But I can't do that if I don't know where he is. This was the last place he appeared. Someone here has to know something."

Lire shrugged, looking unconcerned. "As I've already told you, Jonathan is busy, and neither of my mates nor I have seen him since we left you alone in the guest room."

Eirik pinched the spot between his eyes, trying his ass off to hang onto his calm. Celeste would probably frown upon him leveling her grandson's home.

Kallus took over. "What about Evan? I can smell the dog. Was he with Baptiste?"

A bland smile touched Lire's lips. "That's something else you'll have to discuss with one of the kings. They decide who stays and who goes," he added pointedly.

Eirik's desire to scream doubled when Lire closed the door in his face. Rather than kicking the door in, Eirik turned and hauled Kallus against him. With Kallus wrapped in his arms, and his lips pressed Kallus' forehead, Eirik breathed through the pain.

"We'll find him," Kallus said as he held Eirik tighter.

"Tell me what other choice I had. I swear I saw none."

Kallus' grip tightened on Eirik's shirt. "You tell me and I'll tell you. I didn't know what else to do either."

"You could've trusted him."

"Holy shit," Kallus yelled, jumping away and patting his racing heart.

Jonathan floated above them. The gentle flap of his wings, keeping him hovering just out of reach.

"Hiya," he said when he saw he had Kallus and Eirik's attention.

Eirik growled at the intrusion. "What the fuck? How long have you been spying?"

"First off, this is my house," Jonathan reminded him before softly landing next to them. "Secondly, I don't have to spy. I already know everything. Third, I was trying something that literally has nothing to do with you. D, I don't care enough to listen in on your conversation. And five, you're not the boss of me."

"Dear Odin," Eirik said, shaking his head. "That made zero sense."

"Well, now you know how you sounded blasting off that spying nonsense. Now what do you want?"

Eirik wanted to stamp his feet like a child. He'd never dealt with more infuriating people, and he was the prince of wolves. Those creatures knew how to get under the skin. He counted to ten inside his head. "Baptiste has disappeared. We're trying to find him and were hoping you'd help."

Jonathan's golden gaze moved between them. "Why?"

"So we can work things out," Eirik snapped, incapable of playing nice.

Jonathan shook his head. "That's not what I meant. Why do you need my help?"

"This was the last place his energy appeared before he masked it again," Kallus said, saving Eirik from snapping again. "Plus, Evan's scent is all over this place."

"Evan helped with patrols today," Jonathan said, killing Eirik's hope that Baptiste wasn't alone. He didn't need protection. Baptiste needed companionship. His soul needed the comfort of others. "But I should think, for you, he would be easy to find," Jonathan said, restoring Eirik's hope.

"So you know where he is, then?"

Jonathan immediately killed Eirik's excitement. "No, but you do, if you think about it. You know him better than anyone. What do you know? Baptiste loved you both. He loved being in love with you. The man thrives on your memories and the idea of your union. My guess is, he'll find someplace he feels close to you both while he works on learning to live without you."

Before Eirik could respond, Kallus spoke up. "Why do you keep talking about Baptiste's love like it's a thing of the past?"

"Well," Jonathan said, dragging out the word and glancing between them. "You left," he said, pointing at Kallus. He poked his finger in Eirik's direction, adding, "And you pretended to be dead. Is he supposed to love people forever even when they don't stay? I swear, every immortal I've met would never make it as a human. Humans have short lives. They don't have time for this type of bullshit. I applaud him for leaving. He gave you everything and mourned like a good husband should once you were gone, but three years have passed. The only people who blame him for moving on are the two of you, and neither of you deserve that privilege." Jonathan took a step back and looked up. "Now, if you'll excuse me, I'm still trying something." Jonathan's feet lifted from the ground. His wings were silent and gave off no wind, surprising Eirik with their power. "Good luck finding Baptiste. I genuinely hope you find him and convince him to come back. It hurts me to think I'll never see him again." Without waiting for them to respond, Jonathan disappeared.

"Yeah, me too," Eirik said. Baptiste was powerful. Eirik would never stop looking for him, but if Baptiste wanted, he could stay hidden forever beneath a shield of magic. The thought of never holding Baptiste again; it was hell. He exchanged glances with Kallus. They were thinking the same thing. If this was a quarter of what Baptiste felt at losing them, his pain was unfathomable.

8

Baptiste watched Evan trying to pounce on butterflies from his spot among the flowers. There was no one for hundreds of miles. He'd chosen the most secluded spot he could find, in the same field he'd first made love to Eirik, to set up a new home. It had taken him close to an hour to build up enough magic to craft the perfect two-room cabin, transport Evan's belongings from Jonathan's, and then set up a bubble, keeping them hidden from sight. No one could find them—god nor man, plus anything in between. It had been two weeks since Baptiste set eyes on his mates. In that time, he hadn't found peace, but he'd come to terms with his new reality.

Watching Evan as he played in wolf form helped some. It was obvious Evan had suffered while trapped in the city. Seeing him free made Baptiste feel like he hadn't completely failed at everything he'd touched these past few weeks.

"I'm sorry," Baptiste said, breaking the silence. "If I'd known the truth, I never would have forced you to stay indoors."

Evan didn't slow in his pursuit of a giant yellow butterfly. *It was my choice.* The words sounded winded as they floated through Baptiste's mind. *Mammon killed my pack when I was seventeen. I was the only who survived.* Evan raced by, going in the opposite direction, making Baptiste bite back a laugh despite Evan's confession. *Eirik tried putting me with the Swedish pack so I wouldn't be alone, but I didn't fit in. Aha!* Evan's triumphant cry turned into a groan as the butterfly slipped away again, forcing him to resume his chase.

"What do you mean 'tried'? Why didn't it work out?"

Evan dropped to his belly and switched to stalking mode. *Bleidd was always like, "You need to calm down. You're very sexy, but you need to grow up." I'm grown. I just like to have fun, but Bleidd doesn't believe in fun. His pack is a no-fun zone.*

Baptiste vaguely remembered Bleidd. He was the silver-haired leader of the Sweden pack. "Bleidd said you were sexy? That doesn't sound like someone not fitting in."

Evan trotted over and dropped his head in Baptiste's lap. *Actually, in a pack, that's the definition of not fitting in. Pack leaders are supposed to find mates, breed, and keep the bloodline strong. Finding me sexy wasn't working out for him.*

Baptiste swiped his hands through Evan's fur, finding a sliver of happiness in the sensation of the soft locks sliding across his palms. "What about you? Was it working out for you? From what I recall, Bleidd is a powerful and attractive man."

I'm not strong like you. I'll never land an alpha. Evan's claim shocked Baptiste speechless. *Well, there was this one time I had a moment of bravery. Bleidd was lecturing me about acting like a man, and I kissed him. I mean, that took some courage.* A wave of sadness overcame Baptiste. Baptiste had been unhappy for so long it took him a minute to realize it wasn't his emotions, but Evan's he felt. *For a moment, he kissed me back, but then he shoved me away and said he thought I wasn't a good fit for his pack. I didn't even stand up for myself. I just left. Then, Celeste offered me an escape, and I took it. You shouldn't apologize for taking me away. There was nothing left for me in Sweden.*

Baptiste continued stroking Evan's fur as he

thought over everything Evan said. "I'm not strong," Baptiste admitted, needing to be as honest with Evan as Evan had been with him. "If I was, I wouldn't have lost my mates. They would've trusted me enough to stay with me. Instead of hiding from me so I wouldn't get hurt."

That's not true, Evan argued, sounding vehement. *They had to stay hidden because you're too brave. Eirik and Kallus knew—like everyone did—if they'd stayed, you wouldn't have stopped hunting Mammon until you'd torn out his throat or forced the demon to kill you. As things are, the pain has sort of crippled you, keeping you in the last home you shared with them.*

Baptiste shook his head. "That's not how things seemed to me."

Evan sat back on his haunches. Somehow, his wolf face managed to show the same excitement as the voice filling his head. *That's ridiculous. Everyone's heard the story. Even me, and I was a loner after Bleidd kicked me out.*

"What story?"

Another butterfly floated by, sending Evan into a frenzy. *The story of Mammon kidnapping Kallus. Everyone searched for him, but he was blocked somehow.*

Baptiste shook his head. "I don't remember. Not all of my memories have returned yet."

Evan pounced on a flower. *Well, I remember. No one could find him, but somehow you did. Kallus said you burst through the door like KABOOM.* Evan punctuated the yell with some form of wolfy karate kick, pulling a laugh from Baptiste. As if driven by the sound, Evan raced in circles, burning off excess energy building from the upcoming full moon. *He said you were like, "Hands off my man, you filthy fucker," and you blasted his ass against the wall. You killed like eight demons by yourself, before Mammon got the drop on you, and tied you to a chair with ropes infused with wards burned into the threads. You were badass.* Evan made his way back to Baptiste's side and dropped into his lap, squashing Baptiste's legs with his massive weight. He yawned and already sounded half asleep when he spoke again. *You see, they had to stay hidden. Otherwise, you wouldn't have stopped fighting, and they're not strong enough to lose you the way you lost them.* Evan fell silent for so long Baptiste thought he'd fallen asleep, until his voice floated through Baptiste's head once more, sounding sad. *I didn't fight for Bleidd. Maybe I would've won him, but now, I'll never know. He's probably found his mate. It's hard knowing you'll always be alone. That you don't fit in.*

Baptiste's throat swelled. He knew that feeling

well. "You're not alone. I won't let you be. You're my family now. I'll never leave you."

Evan pressed his head to Baptiste's chest, snuggling close. *It's okay if you do. Everyone goes away eventually. Accepting me as I am is more than anyone else has ever given me.*

With his arms wrapped around Evan's neck, Baptiste hugged the wolf close. Maybe when Evan fell asleep, he'd pop over to Sweden and castrate a wolf. Anger with Bleidd gave Baptiste something else to focus on. No one hurt the people he loved. He urged Evan off his lap and settled on his side next to him. They snuggled together, letting the sun and breeze wash over them. They felt connected in a way he hadn't experienced in a long time. There was an odd tug at his heart when he held Evan.

Baptiste pressed his ear to the ground. Heimdall, Eirik's father, was said to be able to hear every blade of grass as it grew. Baptiste wondered if Eirik could hear his heart beating in the first place they'd made love. He was weak when it came to his mates. As his fingers ran through Evan's fur and his eyelids grew heavy, memories of a different cuddling session overcame him.

A feather brushed along Baptiste's jaw. Damn, the things Kallus had done with that feather. They'd mastered the art of making love without touching. Long ago, they'd learned to stroke and penetrate with inanimate objects—to be in the right place to taste the other's cum. They'd figured out how to kiss with only a magic-infused sheet separating their lips—how to make love with their cocks brushing and that same sheet slipping between their bodies.

Now here they were—Baptiste's back against Eirik's hard chest. That sheet keeping Baptiste safe as Kallus played footsie with him beneath the covers. That goddamn feather brushed his cheek. Fuck, they were his version of heaven. Kallus might be a demon, but he looked like an angel. The man was so damn beautiful. Baptiste's throat swelled each time he looked at him.

"I love you," Baptiste said, not bothering to whisper. Eirik always slept like the dead. He knew they wouldn't disturb him.

"I love you too."

Baptiste's heart skipped a beat at Kallus' claim. It didn't matter they'd been together forever. Their feelings were stronger because of the length of their union.

Kallus shifted, pillowing his head on his arm before settling back down. "You knew I was inside you the moment I possessed you, didn't you?"

It was funny. He would've thought, that after a thousand years, they would've talked about everything there was to talk about. They never spoke of the time Kallus possessed him before they fell in love. "Yes, I knew."

"Why didn't you expel me?"

Baptiste settled deeper into the safety of Eirik's arms and thought about the question. "I guess, growing up in my religion, we're taught nothing, or no one is completely bad or good. Maybe we're more so one or the other, but that's something that's determined by our expectations and experiences. You didn't feel bad. Like me, you felt lonely." A smile pulled at Baptiste's lips. "I'd always been shy and odd, but with you inside me, I didn't feel that way."

"You're the most courageous person I know," Kallus said, taking him by surprise. "Most people hear the word demon and freak. You had one inside you and chose to embrace the power."

Heat filled Baptiste's cheeks. "It didn't hurt that you drove me to do some extremely delicious things to my body when we were alone."

Kallus sucked in a deep breath. Heat filled his gaze. "You've always been amazing. I wanted to feel everything while inside you. Your every response was mind blowing. Still is," Kallus said, inching closer. He made sure the sheet covered every place they touched before cupping Baptiste's erection through the blanket.

The demon's overheated skin had Baptiste sucking in a breath.

Eirik's cock stirred behind him, as if their lust penetrated his dreams. Baptiste chuckled. "We've woken the beast."

A wicked smile touched Kallus' lips as his body became like smoke. "I say let's dredge up some of that kink and play with Eirik. Together, I'm willing to bet we could convince him to do anything." Baptiste absorbed Kallus, taking him inside before rolling and palming Eirik's dick. Together, they could do anything, even own a god.

A tear rolled from the corner of Baptiste's eye before falling into the grass below. He wished the memories would stop coming. They only served to remind him of all he'd never have again.

Evan turned his head as if he smelled Baptiste's tears. He licked Baptiste's eyes, as if trying to kiss them away. A chuckle escaped Baptiste. Maybe he would never be happy again, but that didn't mean he couldn't help Evan.

"How do you feel about going on a trip?"

I'm with you wherever you go.

"Good. We'll have so much fun seeing the world."

Evan settled back down with his head on

Baptiste's chest. *I loved Sweden. Everything about it was beautiful. The water. The trees.*

The wolf named Bleidd, Baptiste silently added to Evan's list. A smile pulled at Baptiste's lips. It was good Evan felt that way since that was exactly where he intended to go.

IT HAD BEEN TWO WEEKS. TWO OF THE LONGEST fucking weeks of Eirik's life. He'd always known there was a good reason he didn't piss off Baptiste. When the man dug his heels in, there wasn't a damn thing he could do. He stared at the sunlight streaming through the window, casting a glow across the comforter of the bed he shared with Kallus inside Dante's house. Since they had nowhere else to go, the vampire had taken them in. They were both sick at heart. Their suffocating emotions filled the room. Kallus didn't sleep. In truth, Eirik didn't need to sleep either, but he still enjoyed doing so. It was an escape. His brain would go elsewhere, creating new places or revisiting old ones. His mental connection with Baptiste had strengthened since their recent blood exchange. Even though Baptiste had him blocked from finding or speaking to him, it seemed when the man slept, the memories that unlocked inside Baptiste's head bombarded Eirik. He couldn't stop waiting for each one. They had so many amazing memories together, he'd forgotten more than he remembered. But he was taking Jonathan's clue to heart. He could still feel Baptiste's love, and he was the type to stay somewhere he could be close to their best memories.

Kallus' warm lips touched the spot between Eirik's shoulder blades. "Do you think he still has that magic-infused sheet he made for us?" He paused for a moment before adding, "I guess we don't need it any longer."

"He still sleeps with it," Eirik said, trying to lift Kallus' spirits, even if he couldn't do anything for his own. "But you're right, he has that necklace from Celeste now. You're free to live a normal life with us."

"That's not what I meant," Kallus said, sounding broken. "I don't think he'll ever choose to touch me again. When I was at Jonathan's, I found myself hoping he'd put me down. I'm very tired, Eirik. Baptiste and you are better when I'm not around."

Eirik rolled. His gaze moved over Kallus' face. He meant it. Kallus was exhausted. "I've failed you too. When Baptiste asked if I'd gone to you, I realized how lacking I've been."

Kallus set his hand on Eirik's cheek. His gaze moved over Eirik's face. "No. I had to keep my father's attention elsewhere. He had to think, if I knew where the key was located, it was nowhere near Baptiste. You've already died once because of me. There's no way you can know how that's broken me. And my little mouse." Kallus rolled to his back and stared at the ceiling. "Fuck, where is he?"

"Somewhere believing we don't really need him," Eirik said, thinking he might choke on the words.

Kallus crossed his arms over his chest. "If you wanted to feel close to us, where would you go?"

Eirik thought it over—like he hadn't turned that exact question over in his mind a thousand times. "Not here," he said without hesitation. "We've only been here about a hundred and fifty years. Baptiste preferred this town because his magic was embraced. When I think about our life together, only two places stand out—where we met in Rouen and Öland."

Kallus shook his head. "I don't think he'd return to the cabin, since that's where he left us. Rouen has changed too much since we left. It doesn't strike me as somewhere Baptiste would go. He likes for things to be silent when he's upset."

"Dear Odin, do you remember that flower field?

Damn, we must have—" Kallus pounced, covering his mouth with his and swallowing Eirik's reminiscing. The pain in his chest was almost unbearable. He wanted his life back. The three of them had been so perfect together. He'd been so damn close to having everything again. Eirik was a warrior. He didn't know how to fix this.

Kallus pulled away and met his stare. "He thinks we don't need him. How do we prove him wrong?"

A smile that felt evil, even to Eirik, pulled at the corners of his lips. "By needing him."

"Exactly," Kallus said, rolling from the bed. "Get up. We have work to do."

The first hint of hope fired to life in Eirik's chest. If Kallus had a plan, Eirik was on board. After all, they had nothing else to lose.

9

This is Sweden. We're in Sweden. Evan hopped in circles around Baptiste, acting more like a fox than a wolf, and making him laugh.

"You said you like it here, and I have a cabin here, so surprise." They walked through the woods, heading toward Baptiste's cabin by the river. He could've zapped them inside the building, but he didn't know if Eirik had set the perimeter alarms. Not to mention, this was such a beautiful place. Baptiste had decided that reconnecting with the earth and taking back his Druid origins would be the best thing for his soul. Each day he spent plugged into nature, his powers grew stronger. He'd let Eirik's death weaken him. For way too long, he'd wasted his magic on minor spells for humans.

Evan ran ahead, pawing at the dirt. A large silver wolf pounced from between the trees, sliding to a stop in front of Evan. He transformed, becoming a large, nude male with silver hair. "What are you doing here, Evan? You were told to leave."

Before Evan could respond, Baptiste threw off the magic shielding him, revealing himself. "What are you doing admonishing my guard?" Bleidd's appearance gave Baptiste an outlet for his rage.

Bleidd immediately gave a short bow. "Baptiste. I didn't see you."

Damn, he really is gorgeous, isn't he? I don't think I can be blamed for my stupidity.

Baptiste bit the inside of his cheek to keep from laughing at Evan's words brushing his mind. He had to keep a straight face. "You didn't see me, because I didn't want to be seen. I brought Evan to the cabin to enjoy some fresh air and to bask in the upcoming full moon."

"I didn't know you were coming," Bleidd said, sounding thoughtful.

Baptiste was really sick of men thinking they had any right to know his whereabouts at all times. "That's because I don't need your permission nor am I required to inform you of anything. I have Evan to watch after me. Which reminds me, don't ever speak to him like that again. As my personal guard, he ranks way higher than you on the food chain. I'm sure you know the punishment for disrespecting the guardian of a god's mate." Baptiste prayed Bleidd knew, and also hoped that it was bad, because he honestly had no clue what the punishment was. Damn, maybe Evan had a point about him being too brave. Ugh. He was so fucking angry at everyone. If Bleidd wanted to fight, Baptiste was ready to throw down with the wolf.

Bleidd dipped his chin, accepting the reprimand as his due. "I apologize. It won't happen again."

Is it petty of me how happy I feel right now? Kiss me and then put me out. Fucker. I should bite his dick off. I would too if it wasn't so pretty.

Bleidd's gaze slid Evan's way, and he covered himself with his hands. "You do realize I can hear you, right?"

Evan went still—like he thought if he didn't as much as blink, then no one would be able to see him. *Actually, no. No, I did not know that.*

Baptiste bit his cheek harder, tasting blood. He moved to Evan's side and rubbed the wolf's head, showing his complete support. "If you'll excuse us," Baptiste said, stepping around Bleidd, as if he didn't matter. They took two steps away, and Baptiste cloaked himself in magic once more. Evan looked back. Baptiste ran his hand down the wolf's neck. "Don't look back, gorgeous. Never let another man's fear steal your happiness. He would be lucky to have you."

Evan whimpered. *That ass, though.*

"All six feet five inches of it," Baptiste said, chuckling. "Seriously, you're too good for someone too weak to claim you."

I love you. As Evan made the claim, he leaned his weight against Baptiste's legs.

For the first time in a long time, Baptiste thought he might survive with nothing more than the love of his friends. "I love you too. Come on. It's getting dark. I'll hang out at the cabin and you can go play in the moonlight."

Baptiste smiled as Evan raced ahead, as if overjoyed at the idea. He'd made the right choice coming here.

Jonathan sat on his hands and stared at the two men sitting across from him. "I'm sorry. You want me to do what?"

Eirik looked serious. "We've caused three years

of suffering to our mate. You need to take us into custody."

The man's words hadn't changed since the last time he'd spoken them, but Jonathan was having a hard time accepting them. He'd spent the last two-and-a-half weeks enjoying the peace and quiet. No one had stopped by unannounced or otherwise. He'd gotten a chance to practice his flying moves, because he totally intended to pull some freaky and kinky moves out for Niall, Cin, and his anniversary. Fuck hanging from a ceiling fan. He could fly.

Now, here Eirik and Kallus sat, suggesting something that was doomed to land him across Niall's lap with the man's palm stinging his... "I'm in," Jonathan said, shifting to his feet. "Come on. I'll have to put you in a different room this time, since you broke all my old wards and cracked my walls while you were at it," Jonathan said, tossing an admonishing look over his shoulder.

Kallus was too busy eyeing each room as they passed to notice, but Eirik grimaced. "I'll pay for the damages."

Jonathan shook his head and looked away. "Don't worry over it. Faolan's an expert at fixing walls. You should've seen our living room after the..." Jonathan snapped his teeth together. No need to tell that story. "Anyhow, we've got it covered."

I need help drawing wards that'll hold a demon, god, and Druid.

Jonathan put the call out, hoping at least one of the guys could help him. Otherwise, he'd be at it all night. To his surprise, everyone appeared to do their part. Eirik even gave some suggestions on how to make their traps as solid as possible.

Once he had Kallus and Eirik on lockdown, he stood back to eye their work. "Now all we have to do is hope Baptiste comes for you. You might be here a while."

Kallus' mouth fell open. "Do you mean you were being serious about not knowing where he is?"

Jonathan spent a moment wondering if the request to lock them down and all the work he'd put into it had been an attempt to get him to come clean about where Baptiste was hiding. "I'm not a liar. He didn't tell me where he was going."

Eirik massaged Kallus' shoulders and pulled him back against his chest. "Don't worry, sexy. Bleidd contacted me earlier. He spotted Baptiste at the cabin and he's been keeping watch to ensure he doesn't get away."

Kallus shot an irritated glance over his shoulder. "You've known this all day and didn't say anything?"

Not an ounce of guilt marred Eirik's features. "If I'd said anything, you would've wanted to head straight there. The moment Baptiste set eyes on us, he'd disappear again, and we'd be right back where we started. This is better."

Jonathan nodded his agreement. "I'll send word to Bleidd to deliver a message for me. This is our best shot at luring him out." Every word Jonathan spoke felt like complete bullshit. There was a big part of him that expected Baptiste wouldn't take the bait. Eirik and Kallus seemed positive Baptiste would come if they were in need. He didn't share their faith. Jonathan loved his mates. That was the only true reason he was going along with this plan. He hoped—if the shoe was on the other foot— they'd go just as far for him to win back his loves. There was no time like the present to get this shit show on the road. All Jonathan could hope was that Baptiste wouldn't hate him after this.

BAPTISTE TILTED HIS HEAD BACK AND STARED AT THE moon. He wondered what it looked like where Eirik and Kallus were. For not the first time, he wondered what would happen if he could possess Kallus the way the man had done to him. He missed the way his men looked at him. Evan's story about the night Eirik died, and his claims of Baptiste's mates not being strong enough to live without him, ate at Baptiste. Eirik had pretended to be someone else to stay close to him. Kallus had invaded his mind, tormenting him. In their own ways, the pair had been incapable of staying away. In truth, he wasn't so sure he would be able to do it forever either.

His feet were cold. It was such a ridiculous thing to be undermining him, but he missed having someone warming his feet. He longed for nights of doing nothing while Eirik massaged his temples. Baptiste would curl up in his lap and listen to stories of Eirik's life. As the guardian of the door between worlds, he'd seen and done so much. All those stories had been stolen from him between Eirik and Celeste's blocking his mind. He wasn't sure if he had them back yet. Baptiste wanted to ask, but there was no one there. The silence inside his mind was deafening.

Evan appeared from between the trees. At the edge of the porch, he transformed from wolf to man. He wrapped a blanket Baptiste had left for him around his waist and sat down on the steps. Baptiste kept himself hidden from everything and everyone but Evan for fear Eirik had the wolves on the lookout for him. No one could see him or hear him but Evan.

"Did you have fun?"

Evan turned sideways at Baptiste's question and leaned his back against the railing. Even though he faced Baptiste, his gaze stayed locked on the nearby trees. "I don't know that 'fun' would be the word I'd use. Mostly, I just walked around, enjoying the silence. Everyone here knows Bleidd banished me, so you know. It's awkward."

Baptiste wished he knew how to make things better. Caring about someone who didn't care back was like dying while still alive. "I'd hoped Bleidd learning you are my guard would ease your way with the local wolves."

Evan shrugged. "It might. I steered clear of the other wolves."

There was nothing Baptiste could think to say to ease Evan. He too was socially inept. Baptiste didn't know how to fit in or how to guide anyone else. "You're incredibly brave to come here and be the lone wolf." Evan's gaze slid his way, as if hanging on Baptiste's every word, so Baptiste didn't stop. "They need each other. You need no one. They'll never know your depth of strength. You should be proud."

Evan didn't respond. His gaze shot to the tree line. He moved to his feet, sending Baptiste on alert. Bleidd stepped into view, wearing nothing, as usual.

"Jeez. This guy again," Baptiste bitched.

Evan held his silence.

"I need to speak with Baptiste," Bleidd said as he moved to a step below Evan, making them the same height.

"He's not accepting visitors tonight," Evan said, keeping his voice hard against Bleidd.

Bleidd glanced around as if searching for any sign Baptiste might be near. His gaze moved back to Evan. His tone softened. "Listen, about earlier, I was just surprised to see you."

Evan looked away and focused on some point over Bleidd's shoulder. "I'm sure."

Baptiste couldn't stop watching the scene play out. Evan's hurt was plain to see for anyone paying attention. Bleidd was more than interested. He couldn't stop eyeing every inch of Evan.

"I'm a leader here."

"Yep," Evan said, making Baptiste proud with his disinterested tone. "I'm aware."

"It's my duty to keep the pack strong."

Evan rocked back on his heels. "So you've said."

Bleidd didn't let up. "I have great, great, great grandchildren older than you."

"That's nice," Evan said, looking away.

Bleidd shifted closer, nosing at Evan's neck.

Evan flattened his palm against Bleidd's chest and pushed. "I'm not accepting visitors tonight either."

"You smell different," Bleidd said, not budging. "Like the city."

"What do you want, Bleidd?" Evan asked, letting his hand slip away from Bleidd's chest in such a way he got an extra feel.

"I saw that," Baptiste said with a chuckle.

Bleidd took a step back. "I have a message for Baptiste from the Americas king."

Baptiste tossed off his magic, revealing his presence. "What's the message?"

Bleidd's gaze moved to where Baptiste sat in a nearby chair. He didn't look surprised to see him. "Eirik and Kallus have been taken into custody. Your presence is requested."

"What?" Evan said, sounding every bit as confused as Baptiste felt.

"I'm not sure that's actually legal, to be honest. Since Eirik is a god, I wouldn't think

Jonathan has any authority over him. I mean, Celeste—"

"Has authorized their detainment," Bleidd said, cutting him off.

"What?" Evan repeated, obviously every bit as lost as Baptiste.

Eirik was the guardian of the door between worlds. It wasn't as if he could be detained, right? Baptiste shook his head. "I'll go," Baptiste said. He might be confused and angry, but his mates needed him.

Evan wrapped his blanket tighter around his waist. "I'll go with you and watch your back."

Baptiste shook his head. "Stay. Enjoy the night. This won't take long. An hour, at most."

He could see the worry in Evan's eyes—like he expected Baptiste to abandon him the way everyone did. "Okay."

As if Evan was still in wolf form, Baptiste stroked the man's hair. "Don't worry. I'll be back soon."

Evan nodded, and Baptiste disappeared. He landed on Jonathan's porch and rang the bell. He was tempted to zap inside, stamping all over their rules of propriety. For heaven's sake, they'd taken his mates into custody. Fuck manners. The door opened, and Dougal stared out. His jaw was set in a hard line.

"Baptiste, come in. Jonathan is waiting for you."

The ominous feel of the house had Baptiste on edge and doubled his confusion. He'd thought they'd found a modicum of friendship. "What's going on? Bleidd said my mates were detained."

Dougal tossed a glance over his shoulder as he led Baptiste down the hall. "Aye, earlier today. Jonathan will explain everything."

"That makes no sense. Eirik is a god."

"Aye, I know."

Jonathan came into view. He looked more powerful than usual tonight, standing outside the same guest bedroom where Baptiste had his last argument with is mates. No friendship marred the man's features. He was the Nephilim—the grandson of Goddess Celeste tonight.

"Baptiste," Jonathan said, dipping his chin.

Lire and Faolan appeared behind him before he could respond. He felt trapped in the narrow hallway with Jonathan and Dougal blocking one way and Faolan and Lire blocking the other, especially when he felt a wave of weariness overcome him. He wasn't tired. It was more of a draining of power. Symbols on the walls glowed orange, making him realize the king had him trapped, draining his magic.

"What the fuck?" Baptiste growled. His rage grew.

Jonathan opened the door beside him and waved Baptiste inside. "I've recaptured Kallus from his earlier escape, and Eirik has been brought in for interfering with king's business."

Baptiste strolled inside and found his mates pacing the floor, trapped behind a wall of invisible magic. The level of Baptiste's fury at seeing his mates caged like animals was enough to bring down the house. His powers were dampened. He couldn't fight. Not to mention, this was Jonathan. He was a reasonable man.

"Let them go. You said it was my place to judge them. Let them go. That's what I want."

For a moment, Jonathan looked sad. "I'm sorry, Baptiste. That was the case before, but now you're equally guilty of abandonment. All three of you will stay until you've come to a mutual agreement."

"What?" His brain wouldn't work.

"Hopefully, you won't be here long," Jonathan said with a sad smile. "I don't like this either," he added. "You're a good man, and I'd like to think we're friends, but I'm a king first."

He turned, as if ready to leave. Horror overcame Baptiste. He scrambled after Jonathan. "Wait. Hold up. Evan will think I abandoned him. Don't do that to me. Everyone else has already left him." Jonathan turned at his plea.

"Told you I smelled the dog," Kallus said behind him.

Baptiste ignored him and didn't let up. "Please? I left him in Sweden at our cabin. I promised him I'd be right back. If I don't show, he'll be heartbroken. Evan is so young and sweet. He won't understand. He doesn't deserve that level of cruelty of being dropped like a stray." He had to make Jonathan understand. "I can't do that to him. I can't do what was done to me."

"But you did," Jonathan pointed out. His voice was soft, as if expected to spook Baptiste, or hoped to soothe his panic even as he admonished him. "You walked away from your mates with every intention of not coming back."

A swift denial raced to Baptiste's lips. It didn't fall, but realization struck. He was furious with the men standing at his back. But, in his heart, he never intended to stay gone. He'd only wanted them to taste what he had. Baptiste had needed them to understand the hopelessness. They had to feel what he'd felt, or he'd never forgive them. He'd never look at them the same.

Jonathan patted his shoulder. "Don't worry about Evan. I'll fetch him in an hour, if you haven't come to terms by then."

Relief washed over Baptiste. Evan would come and know his importance. When the door closed, leaving Baptiste with nothing else to focus upon, he took a breath. Even to his ears, the life-giving oxygen passing his lips sounded ragged. He turned and tried eyeing everything except his mates. The wooden bedframe was still cracked from Niall and his abuse. Kallus sat on the edge of the bed. Baptiste's gaze skirted over him and landed on the cherry wood dresser. It had a mirror hanging over it. Eirik stood, leaning against the piece. Fuck. There was no safe place to look. No one said anything, making the situation twice as awkward.

"Come here," Kallus said.

Baptiste's gaze automatically shot his way. The hard set to Kallus' jaw said he wouldn't tolerate disobedience. The hurt in his eyes said it would break him if Baptiste refused. The combination had Baptiste's feet moving in his direction. He stopped just out of Kallus' reach. Kallus held his hand out to Baptiste. Baptiste looked between his beautiful blue eyes and the outstretched hand. He was temptation's bitch.

"Please?"

Baptiste reached out and stroked the tips of Kallus' fingers. They were so hot. Baptiste wanted more. His palm slid across Kallus's. A sharp breath escaped Kallus, forcing Baptiste's eyes up. Kallus stared at their hands, looking like he expected the worst while praying for the best. There was so much desperation in his eyes. His fingers closed around Baptiste's hand. He tugged, pulling Baptiste closer until Baptiste stood between his knees. Kallus touched his lips to the back of Baptiste's hand and held it there. Baptiste couldn't look away. Kallus swallowed so hard Baptiste heard it happen. He felt the man's lips shape into a smile before falling again against his skin.

"So many times over the years, I've just wanted to hold your hand."

The backs of Baptiste's eyes stung at Kallus' confession. A drop of water so hot it scalded his skin landed on Baptiste's hand before rolling away. It took Baptiste a moment to realize it was a tear. Baptiste found himself shuffling closer. He wasn't the type to intentionally hurt anyone. It made him sick to think of his mates hurting. Baptiste's heart hurt, and he was exhausted.

"You could've been holding my hand for three years now, if you hadn't walked away."

Kallus shook his head and brushed his lips across the back of Baptiste's hand. "I'm the reason Mammon knew how to bind you to that chair." Baptiste stared at the top of Kallus' head and tried working through the man's words. Thankfully, Kallus didn't force him to question the confession. His gaze met Baptiste's gaze and Baptiste couldn't look away from the pain in Kallus' eyes. "While being tortured, I tried giving him enough to make the pain stop, while not giving him enough to harm either of you." Kallus visibly swallowed. "He has ways... I don't know how to fix that betrayal. You could've died because of me. Eirik *did* die because of me. I don't deserve to hold your hand."

Baptiste cupped Kallus' jaw. "Everything that's happened, happened because of Mammon and no one else. I'm a man too. I get that we act and don't talk things out." Baptiste pushed his words through a rapidly swelling throat. "I understand you don't want to tell me about the three days with Mammon when I couldn't find you, but if you'd spent five minutes with me, you would've known how I feel about things." Baptiste moved closer, and Kallus wrapped his arms around his waist, holding on. He held Kallus' jaw, ensuring the man couldn't look away. "You would've known, I just wanted you to come home. I had to go to bed every night and wake up every morning, knowing the last time I saw you, you were half alive."

"I didn't—"

"Shhh," Baptiste said, trying to have his say for once. "It doesn't matter why you chose to stay away, you still chose to stay away. Celeste gave me this," he said, pulling the necklace out from inside his shirt and showing it to Kallus. "It's so I can touch you, and that's all I wanted—to hold you and see for myself you were okay. To kiss away any lingering pain."

While holding his gaze, Kallus slowly unbuttoned his shirt until the material hung open. "I'm okay. See? No scars or anything."

Baptiste dropped his gaze to Kallus' chest. His mouth watered, and each breath came a little harder than the last. He pushed the material aside and trailed his fingers along his mate's perfect skin. Demons ran hotter than the average human since they were more energy than solid, leaving them free to possess others. Baptiste had only ever felt Kallus with protective material between them. It was hard to hold on to his anger while finally touching his mate. His throat swelled to the point he couldn't speak.

"I've never thought of you as weak," Kallus said, bringing Baptiste's gaze back to his. No one could see his face and call him a liar.

"Me either," Eirik said, making Baptiste jump when his hands unexpectedly landed on Baptiste's shoulders. Baptiste didn't pull away, even as Eirik's body molded against his back and his arms crossed Baptiste's chest. "I'm the one who's weak. No matter what happens to whatever body I'm in, the gods won't let me die. As long as there is a heaven or a world and a path between them, I will exist. Until I loved you both, I never realized how much that could be a curse. If anything happened to either of you, I'd be trapped—never ceasing to exist with nothing to live for. I saw that horrible fate play out for me when I rushed into that house and saw the two of you bound. You're the strong one," Eirik added. "I've always known you could live without me, blood mated or not."

Everything Evan had said was true. Eirik hadn't meant to make Baptiste feel weak or unimportant. That didn't mean all was forgiven, but damn, he needed a break from the constant pain and anger he'd felt for the past three years. He wasn't over this. That would take time. Baptiste was still furious, but those emotions were dulled with Kallus and Eirik touching him. They were his biggest weakness. There wasn't much he wouldn't do for them, even if it meant swallowing his pain.

The door flew open and Jonathan poked his head inside. "Is everything worked out?" He looked so damn happy and hopeful, Baptiste almost hated to squash his optimism.

Baptiste pushed Kallus' shirt over his shoulders and down his arms. "No," Baptiste said, holding Kallus' gaze. "We're nowhere near coming to terms."

"Okie dokie," Jonathan chirped, slamming the door closed.

The distinct sound of a bolt being thrown filled the room. Then, everything was silent. Only Eirik's breaths brushing his ear broke through the quiet. "Has Eirik checked the rest of your body for scars or lingering injuries yet?" Baptiste asked, as he peeled away Kallus' shirt.

Kallus shook his head. "We've been busy searching for you."

"We should check now. Don't you think?" Eirik asked.

"Demons don't scar, Little Mouse," Kallus said as he sprang, covering Baptiste's mouth with his.

For half a second, Baptiste froze at the unexpected move. His body didn't care what Baptiste thought about the situation. It knew its mate. The moment Kallus' tongue touched the corner of his mouth, Baptiste opened for him. His entire body lit as their tongues met. It was the first time they'd ever been able to kiss like this. He'd always tried hard not to envy Eirik for his freedom with Kallus' body. Now everything was his. Eirik's lips skimmed Baptiste's nape. His short fingernails skimmed Baptiste's sides as he dragged Baptiste's shirt up. Baptiste pulled away from Kallus only long enough for Eirik to pull the material over his head and toss it aside. Then he was back, savoring Kallus's kiss.

Eirik tore at Baptiste's clothes. Baptiste let it happen. He no longer cared about anything beyond the need to connect with the other pieces of his soul. Baptiste went for the button of Kallus' pants. Kallus fell back across the mattress and let Baptiste have his way. For a moment, with Eirik's mouth caressing every new inch of Baptiste's skin he bared, Baptiste had to stop and breathe through the lust.

"Look what I found," Eirik said, sounding

triumphant. "Someone uses this room," he added as he tossed a bottle of lube on the bed next to Kallus.

Baptiste snatched it up. "Good." His gaze met Kallus's. The man looked half crazed with desire. "I'll need this."

"Goddamn," Kallus breathed, sounding every bit as turned on as he appeared.

Baptiste took his time, stripping Kallus bare and oiling the man's asshole. Eirik reached past him, snagged Kallus' legs, and hauled the man to the edge of the bed.

His hot breath brushed Baptiste's ear as he urged Kallus' legs higher. "Fuck him, Little Mouse. He's been waiting for too long, and I'm out of patience." The growled confession nearly buckled Baptiste's knees. Kallus held his stare as Baptiste pushed his way inside. The way the demon bit his lip before gasping, as if in heaven, almost had Baptiste coming. Then, Eirik took control, fingering Baptiste's asshole before impaling him with his cock. Baptiste saw stars. Kallus was twice as hot as any other man would be on his dick. Baptiste needed a moment to center himself but Eirik didn't let him have it. Eirik set their pace. The entire bed rocked, scraping across the hardwood floor as Eirik slammed inside Baptiste, pushing Baptiste deeper inside Kallus.

Baptiste kissed any body part he could reach, losing himself to the moment. It was hot as hell, watching Kallus struggle for air and tug at his cock—like he was crazed from the havoc Baptiste wreaked on his body. Sexy images filled Baptiste's head. He wanted his men's cocks in his mouth. Baptiste craved the sensation of having them fill his ass at the same time. Eirik's fangs pierced his skin without warning. Baptiste cried out. Eirik's grip tightened on Baptiste's throat. An orgasm slammed into him, stealing his every thought. Nothing but the pleasure existed. The ecstasy of Eirik's cock stretching him wide while pops of electricity danced on his dick, forcing him to fill Kallus' ass with cum, was the only thing he knew. He couldn't stop writhing and reaching for more. Scalding hot cum coated his stomach as Kallus' orgasm joined his. Still, even with Kallus' cries bouncing from the walls, Baptiste couldn't stop fucking him.

"You are both *mine*," Eirik growled as he came.

The claim had Baptiste crying out. There was a tug in his chest, letting him know the declaration had been more than just words. Eirik, the god and protector of the gateway, had just demanded recognition of his mates. It had been an open claim in his new form. Nothing could undo those words.

Kallus and he belonged to Eirik. They were a god's mates.

Even after they collapsed into a sweaty, cum-soaked mess, and the cool air dried their skin, Baptiste waited for the regret to rush in. It didn't come. He held tighter to his men, tugging them closer until he could barely breathe. Goddess help him, he loved them more than he loved himself. His eyes burned with unshed tears. There was nothing he wouldn't endure as long as they lived and loved him in return.

Eirik's lips brushed his cheek, as if he felt Baptiste's pain. "Stop thinking, Little Mouse. I love you. If anyone ever comes for us again, I won't make the same mistakes. Nothing breaks this," he said, tightening his hold on them both.

Kallus pressed his forehead to Baptiste's and nodded while holding his gaze. "Never again. I can't ever be separated from either of you again. I can't," he repeated, sounding every bit as broken as Baptiste had felt for the past three years. Baptiste knew then, the suffering hadn't been his alone. He'd wanted to prove he was strong, but—really—all he'd done was prove to himself he was weak. Without these men, he was incomplete. He could exist without them. That he knew, but he couldn't *live* without them, and that wasn't at all the same.

For a long time, they held each other. Even though Baptiste knew he wouldn't sleep, he closed his eyes and held tight. Although he was a Druid and believed in the elements above all else, he still prayed to Odin. He begged the Norse god to keep their union safe from ever dealing with anything like this again. In that bed, while holding his mates, he believed his prayers were heard.

10

The absolute silence penetrated his mind first. Followed closely by the knowledge he had his life back again. Eirik's eyes shot open, needing to see his mates resting beside him. The bed was empty. A shot of fear punched him in the gut. If Baptiste and Kallus were gone, it would kill him. His gaze shot around the room. The wards were broken. Turning inside himself, he searched for any signs of his mates. A smile pulled at the corners of his mouth as he felt them. They were nearby. He could feel them and hear them. Only happy thoughts ruled their minds. For a moment, Eirik didn't move. He basked in their combined glow. The drive to hold them again and kiss them had him throwing the covers back. He rushed through getting dressed.

Faolan flashed him a smile as they passed in the hall as if he wasn't out-of-place in their home. "Your mates are lazing in the moonlight out back." Faolan's claim made him realize he'd slept for more than fifteen hours. The strain of the passing years had gotten the best of him. For the first time in a damn long time, he felt refreshed.

"Thanks. Could you point me in the right direction?"

Faolan sent him through the living room and kitchen and out the back door. He picked up the pace, dying to be close to his everything. Eirik's steps slowed as he stepped outside. He smiled at the sight of Baptiste on the ground with Evan. Evan was in wolf form. Baptiste rubbed both hands through his fur while Evan rested his chin on Baptiste's shoulder. The scene warmed Eirik's heart. Evan hadn't fit in with other wolves. The boy didn't have any family, and he'd been trapped in the city because of Eirik. Kallus relaxed in the grass next to the pair with his hand on Baptiste's leg and his eyes closed.

Baptiste rubbed Evan's ears. "We'll do whatever you want, sweetie," Baptiste said, cooing each word as if trying to soothe Evan. "Do you want me to neuter him? I will. I don't have a single qualm about it."

No. It's not worth it, but I don't want to go back.

"We won't," Baptiste assured him. "I won't make you go back there. Or, just hear me out. I could have him killed, then you can still enjoy the cabin."

I love you.

"I love you too, sweetie," Baptiste said, hugging the wolf tighter.

Eirik blinked several times. Surprise rendered him mute. "Wait." Kallus' eyes shot open at Eirik's loud interruption. He hadn't meant to yell. His shock had taken control of his tongue. "Can you hear him?" Three sets of eyes stared at Eirik as if he'd lost his mind. He motioned toward the wolf crawling all over Baptiste. "Can you hear Evan's thoughts when he's in this form?"

Baptiste went back to petting Evan. "Of course. Can't you?"

"Well, yeah. Wolves fall under my rule. I can hear all wolves." A bright smile pulled at the corners of his mouth. He couldn't help it. "You shouldn't be able to hear him, but you can. Do you know what this means?"

Baptiste didn't seem that interested or anywhere near as excited as he should be. He continued playing with Evan like hearing a wolf's thoughts happened every day. "What does it mean?"

"Odin has recognized you as a warrior and blessed you with a guardian. Evan is your wolf. No matter what, he'll stay with you, even if he finds a mate. He's your family."

Baptiste and Evan froze. "Wait. What?" Baptiste looked Kallus' way. "Can you not hear him?"

"Nope," Kallus said, smiling. "I've just been listening to you baby him and threaten to castrate some wolf that upset him."

Baptiste looked back at Evan. He kissed his furry cheek while smiling brightly. "Did you hear that? I told you I'd never let you be alone."

Evan ran in circles, cheering. Eirik couldn't stop smiling as he moved to sit between his men. Things were looking up. He hadn't had so much hope in a long damn time. After stealing a quick kiss from both his men, Eirik settled down on the grass next to Kallus. A loud sigh escaped him the moment his gaze hit the night sky. Jonathan floated above them beneath the limbs of an oak tree—like the world's largest cherub floating on a cloud. Jonathan gave him a tiny finger wave. "Now you can say I'm a spy."

A bubble of laughter rose in Eirik's throat. It was impossible to be mad at Jonathan. Thank Odin the man was a busybody. Otherwise, Eirik might not be between his men right now with hope for the future.

He'd never forget his debt. As Baptiste curled against his chest, Eirik silently swore he'd find a way to settle up one day.

The End.

KEEP AN EYE OUT FOR THE NEXT BOOK IN THE SERIES, *Hunger.* Book five is Evan's book. It will pick up where Evan was left behind in Sweden, so you don't miss a second of what happened when he was left alone with Bleidd.

ABOUT THE AUTHOR

Charity Parkerson is an award winning and multi-published author with several companies. Born with no filter from her brain to her mouth, she decided to take this odd quirk and insert it in her characters.

*Seven-time Readers' Favorite Award Winner

   *2015 Passionate Plume Award Finalist

   *2013 Reviewers' Choice Award Winner

   *2012 ARRA Finalist for Favorite Paranormal Romance

   *Five-time winner of The Mistress of the Darkpath

Connect with her online:

--Join my street team: facebook.com/TeamCharityParkerson

   --Sign up for my newsletter: http://bit.ly/CharityNews

   --Website: charityparkerson.com

--Facebook:

facebook.com/authorCharityParkerson

facebook.com/TheMenofSin

--Twitter: twitter.com/CharityParkerso

www.ingramcontent.com/pod-product-compliance
Lightning Source LLC
Chambersburg PA
CBHW071722200626
46817CB00021B/2927